Castles and Dragons

COMPILED BY THE

Child Study Association of America

Read-to-Me Storybook

Read Me Another Story

Read Me More Stories

Holiday Storybook

Read to Yourself Storybook

More Read to Yourself Stories:
Fun and Magic

Castles and Dragons

Read to Me Again

Now You Can Read to Yourself

Castles

AND

Dragons

READ-TO-YOURSELF FAIRY TALES
for BOYS and GIRLS

ILLUSTRATED BY
William Pène du Bois

COMPILED BY THE
Child Study Association
of America

THOMAS Y. CROWELL COMPANY · NEW YORK

ACKNOWLEDGMENTS

For permission to reprint the following copyrighted material, grateful acknowledgment and thanks are extended to the sources indicated:

Elizabeth Coatsworth, for "The Story of Wang Li" from *The Cricket and the Emperor's Son,* copyright 1932 by Elizabeth Coatsworth.

Coward-McCann, Inc., for "The Sorcerer's Apprentice" from *More Tales from Grimm* by Wanda Gág, copyright © 1947 by Wanda Gág.

Dodd, Mead & Company, Inc., for "The Good Sword" from *The Castle in the Silver Wood* by Ruth Bryan Owen, copyright © 1939 by Dodd, Mead & Company, Inc.

E. P. Dutton & Company, Inc., for "The King of the Hares" from the book *Cinderella's Mouse and Other Fairy Tales* by Rosalie K. Fry, copyright 1953 by E. P. Dutton & Company, Inc.; and for "The Lost Half-Hour" from the book *Henry Beston's Fairy Tales* by Henry Beston, copyright 1952 by Henry Beston.

Faber & Faber Ltd., The Society of Authors, and The Literary Trustees of Walter de la Mare, for "Ashputtel" from *Animal Stories* by Walter de la Mare.

In dedicating this book to
Elizabeth Riley
the Children's Book Committee expresses
its affectionate gratitude for her inspiration,
unfailing patience, and editorial wisdom
over the years.

CONTENTS

THE fairy tale reaches deep into the inner world of a child, giving substance to his dreams, putting into words his own feelings of wonder and longing.

"I like fairy stories because bad things happen to the bad people and good things happen to the good people and miracles happen to everybody." Thus Penny, aged nine, explained quite simply the lasting appeal of the fairy tale: justice is incorrupted; the youngest, the weakest, and the spurned ones finally win their true loves—and half the kingdom—while the wicked uncle and the scheming prime minister undergo a suitably horrid fate.

Worldly success—the jewels and the castles—may seem to be the reward, yet even young children recognize instinctively that these are but symbols for the power of good. Things come right, not only for those who wish them to, but for those who selflessly strive and serve.

All of us would wish for our children the virtues and graces that endure in fairy tales. Heroines are lovely and endearing; villains are wicked, greedy, and rude. The kitchen drudge and the swineherd are brave and truthful; their rivals, cowardly and churlish. If the goosegirl is the real princess and the woodcutter's son is the real prince, is this not just another way of saying that true nobility is an inward quality?

In the world of fairies there is neither time nor space. A fairy tale begins with "Once upon a time," but what the time is, and what the place, we shall never know. When a mortal steps into this enchanted world, a thousand years are but a day, and he may travel east o' the sun and west o' the moon in the space of a single breath. For the adventures of fairyland are adventures of the child's own fantasy.

From the inexhaustible treasure house of fairy tales we have chosen these stories to bring children some of their own heritage. For the echoes of fairy tales underlie many of our great books, our poetry, and our very language. Culturally and emotionally they prepare young readers for the literature they will enjoy in later years.

The familiar pattern of the fairy tale is universal. The stories selected for this book are faithful to that pattern, though they are far from alike in theme and substance. Each has its own quality in the telling and each its own deep truth. In this book you will not meet Beauty or the Frog Prince or Cinderella, but you will find characters who have the same ageless virtues. Here, too, as in the immortal tales, children learn to suffer and to triumph through others.

Fairy tales speak to the innocent heart in all of us.

The Children's Book Committee *of the*
Child Study Association of America

Castles and Dragons

The Half-Pint Jinni

by MAURICE DOLBIER

IN the years of enchantment, when Haroun-al-Raschid was Caliph of Baghdad and Baghdad was the wonder of the world, there lived a boy named Ali, who dwelt in the house of his uncle in a fishing village on the shores of the Red Sea.

Ali's uncle was a fisherman, but unlike most fishermen of that time he was very well-to-do. He had not always been wealthy. Indeed, he had once been only a ragged beggar. But great good fortune (so he said, and his neighbors believed) had come to him. One day, when he was fishing in the sea, a huge golden fish had leaped into his small boat. This fish had spoken to Ali's uncle in the purest Arabic, begging to be thrown back into the sea. The fish had added to its entreaties a promise to

[*1*]

disclose the hiding place of a great treasure. So, Ali's uncle agreed. The fish told him the site of the treasure, and was hurled back safely to its sea home. And behold! the fish's words were true, and Ali's uncle came upon a great cache of gold and silver, and had been the richest man in the village since that day.

So he said, and so almost all the village believed. Only a few were aware of the truth: that Achmed the Lucky, as he was called, was one of the greatest liars in Arabia and one of the wickedest men.

For while he fished for fish in the day, Achmed and a band of his followers fished for purses in the night, robbing on the roads where the caravans passed.

Ali did not know the night side of his uncle's life, nor share in his uncle's riches. From dawn to dusk, Ali was made the slave of the household. From dusk to dawn, he slept on a straw pallet in a corner of the stable.

And as he slept, he dreamed. Often his dreams were of simple things: of wearing clothes that were not ragged and dirty, of being free to run and play, of being allowed for once to eat until he stopped being hungry. But sometimes his dreams wandered further, and he thought himself a handsome prince, living in a palace in Baghdad and married to the most beautiful princess in the world. In these dreams, he wore robes of gold and scarlet, and dined off silver plates, and had a chorus of minstrels to entertain him, and was the friend and adviser of the Caliph himself. Into these dreams there often entered a shabby beggar, whining for bread, and recognizable, despite his tattered garb and dirty face, as Achmed his uncle. Always in these dreams, Ali himself went to greet the wretched man, and invited him into his palace, and gave him food and drink, and restored his fortunes.

But awakening came, and with it Achmed . . . neither tattered nor wretched, but with a voice like a whip, driving him about the thousand and one tasks of the bitter day.

On one day of the week Ali tasted the air of freedom. On one day only, his uncle granted him the privilege of working at sea. When the little boats scudded across the choppy waters of the bay, and the soft breezes filled the sails, Ali's heart was joyful.

Besides the happiness that came with these spacious days at sea, a hope came, too. Time after time he had heard the storytellers telling of fishermen who drew into their nets great gold-encrusted brass bottles with sealed mouths which, once broken, emitted first a large cloud of smoke and then, rising and towering into the air, monstrous jinn, imprisoned in the ancient years by Suleiman the King, and willing to grant their liberators every wish.

So always, as the great pile of fish spilled out over the deck of the fishing boat, Ali's sharp eyes would seek to catch the glint of gold, and always they saw nothing but fish and fish and more fish. Until one day . . .

The gold flashed!

Ali stooped and thrust his slim brown arm into the wriggling mass of fish. His hand closed on a bottleneck. Carefully, and without being observed by his crew-mates, he drew forth his prize. He sat back on his heels, and frowned as he looked at the bottle. This was not the kind of bottle that appeared in all the marvelous stories. It was a squat, ugly little bottle and it looked most unpromising. Surely, no monstrous jinni could be concealed in this! Nevertheless, Ali slipped it beneath his ragged blouse.

That night, alone in his stable corner, Ali brought forth the bottle and examined it by candlelight. The neck was sealed, and for the first time Ali noticed a string of weird letters winding around the bottle.

With hands that he could not keep from trembling, Ali

broke the seal. Holding his breath, he waited, watching the bottle opening.

Nothing happened.

Ali laughed, a little ashamed of himself for having expected anything to happen. A shabby half-pint bottle. . . .

He lay down on his straw pallet and pursed his lips to blow out the candle. Perhaps in his sleep he would find a magic bottle.

Ali blinked his eyes.

A thin stream of smoke was emerging from the bottle.

He sat up again quickly, and stared.

The smoke spurted toward the ceiling in a long straight line, and then, as he watched, spirals began to form and spread. At last a huge cloud of smoke had formed. Ali's eyes widened in awe. He kept his gaze fixed on the top of the cloud, for this was where, in the stories of the market place, the first sign of a jinni usually appeared . . . the enormous turbaned head, the angry eyes, the fearsome mouth with its ivory fangs. By releasing the monster, he was its master and it was his servant.

But as the minutes passed no monster appeared. The smoke began to break away in wisps and disappear. Once again Ali's hopes had been dashed. Reluctantly he drew his glance away from the vanishing smoke and looked at the bottle itself. And as he looked, he felt the hairs of his head begin to rise.

A tiny jinni, about four inches high, was staring at him. The head was turbaned, and the mouth had its two small ivory fangs in the regular places, but the eyes were not angry. They were as blue as the summer sky, and they looked appealingly at Ali.

"I suppose," said the jinni, "you were expecting something else. I'm not much to look at, I admit."

For a moment Ali wondered. "Are you a jinni?" he asked.

"Oh, yes," said his strange little visitor. "I'm a jinni, all right. Name of Mardak. And bound to be the servant of that fortunate one who breaks the seal and opens the bottle. Happy to oblige."

"You mean you can fulfill my every wish?" asked Ali delightedly.

The jinni squinted a little, and reflectively scratched at one of his teeth.

"That's my trade," he admitted. "Fulfilling wishes. Never had much practice at it. Caught too young, really. But I can try."

Now Ali stood up, and even through his excited plannings he felt a certain sense of the ridiculous. Instead of a jinni looming over him, here he was looming over a jinni.

"Good!" said Ali. "Let me think! What do I wish for most first . . . ?"

The jinni cocked his head.

"Money?" he suggested. "Money's a useful commodity. Buys things."

"I won't need money, will I?" Ali asked. "Because I won't need to buy things. I just ask for things, and you provide them."

"That's so," said the jinni. "My, you're an intelligent youngster! I'd never have thought of that."

"I have it!" said Ali. "First . . . I wish to be robed in silken garments, suitable for a prince."

"Suit of clothes, eh?" said Mardak. "No sooner said than done!"

And he raised his little right arm commandingly into the air, and closed his eyes tightly.

A rather long pause followed, and for a time both of them were afraid that nothing was going to happen. Then the candle flame dwindled and grew bright again, and Ali felt the caress of silk on his shoulders. He looked down,

saw a shimmer of purple, was about to exclaim joyfully, then uttered instead an exclamation of dismay.

From his throat to his waist, the new clothes he wore would indeed arouse the envy of a prince. However, from his waist to his feet, he still wore the usual rags.

The jinni bit his lower lip and wrinkled his brow. "That's an odd thing now," he said. "I went through the proper rigmarole, just the way my old daddy taught me. Let's go at this more slowly. I'll wish a pair of shoes for you. . . . Shoes! Extra fancy! With gold buckles!"

Ali watched his own feet closely. One of them was suddenly encased in an extra-fancy shoe, with a gold buckle. The other remained bare.

Mardak the jinni shook his head.

"This beats me," he said. "It must be because I'm only a half-pint jinni. Apparently I can answer only half your wishes."

A tear welled up in his right eye and rolled down the side of his grotesque little face.

"Wait a minute," said Ali. "It strikes me that there's a simple solution to this."

The jinni looked up, half-hopefully and half-skeptically, as befitted a half-pint jinni.

"Suppose I wished for *two* suits of silken raiment?"

"What a brillant mind you possess," cried Mardak happily. "If I tried for two, I'd be sure of getting one, wouldn't I?"

Mardak raised his arm and shut his eyes. The usual long pause followed, and then . . . there was Ali, the poor fisherboy, clad in silks from throat to ankles, and crowned with a silken turban with a glorious blazing emerald.

"It worked," cried Mardak. "You were right!"

A great feeling of happiness surged over Ali.

"If only I had a mirror," he said. Then added quickly: "I mean, two mirrors."

"Two mirrors!" said the jinni, and one mirror appeared.

Ali, with shining eyes, surveyed his princely reflection in the glass.

"Four shoes," he commanded.

The jinni nodded, and with a self-satisfied grin produced two extra-fancy shoes with golden buckles.

"I'm beginning to enjoy this," he said. "It's fun to give things to people."

He raised his hand, closed his eyes. . . . A jewel-hilted Damascus sword was suddenly swinging at Ali's side. Ali looked down at it in pleased surprise.

"My own idea," said Mardak modestly. "I hope that you like it."

Ali liked the sword very much; he liked the fine clothes and the jewels that the jinni provided in answer to his wishes. But then in the sky of his happiness a cloud appeared. Soon morning would come, and with morning his uncle Achmed. It would be well to be far away from this place before the sun rose.

Blessed by the kindly Fates, the proud possessor of a personal jinni . . . even if only a half-pint one. . . . Ali saw that now the road to freedom was open to him . . . the road that could lead to the fulfillment of his most ambitious dreams . . . the road that led, in the first place, to the golden-domed city of Baghdad.

And so:

"Take me to Baghdad!" he ordered.

A great rushing noise sounded in his ears, and he felt himself being swirled and twirled and whirled and hurled up and up and up, so fast that he could neither breathe nor swallow, and then he felt himself plunging down and down and down . . . until at last he came to rest, with a gentle bump, on the ground. His head seemed to spin for hours, but finally he sat up and looked around.

Under the bright starshine he saw, as far as the horizon on every side, only the long, cold, rolling wastes of a great desert.

"Oh, my," said a shocked little voice beside him. "We completely forgot. We must be only halfway to Baghdad."

"This will take some puzzling," said Ali, wrinkling his brow. "Let's see . . . I wish we were half as far . . . no . . . twice as far . . . no, certainly not! . . . I wish . . . I have it! I wish we were as far from Baghdad on the other side as we are on this."

"That sounds reasonable," said Mardak. "Ready? Hold on. Here we go!"

Again Ali heard the rushing noise and felt himself jouncing and bouncing through the air with the speed of an arrow, and sometimes he saw the stars' bright pattern over his head and sometimes under his feet. And then. . . .

Bump!

Wherever they were, they were not in Baghdad. The desert that surrounded them here was, if anything, harsher, colder and stonier than the one they had just left.

"Oh, what a useless jinni I am!" said Mardak sadly. "Everything I do is wrong. And it's all because Suleiman

William Père du Bois

never let me reach my full growth. I'm more trouble than
I'm worth."

"You mustn't feel that way." Ali consoled him. "This
must be my fault entirely. It's my fault for not putting my
wishes in the proper form. Now . . . what can have gone
wrong this time? I asked to be as far from Baghdad on
this side as we were on the other. . . . Of course! And
that's just what happened! We're only half as far from
Baghdad on this side as we were on the other."

"Well," said Mardak, "we're getting nearer all the
time."

"Perhaps," said Ali, "it would be better, since we're so
near, to reach the city in the ordinary way of travel. Let's
go to Baghdad by camel."

"Now that's something easily produced," said Mardak.
He raised his hand. "You want *two* camels, don't you?"
he asked, and winked.

"Yes," said Ali. "Two camels."

Mardak snapped his fingers. A complete camel appeared, chomping and snuffling as though it had not just
arrived from thin air.

"Now," said Ali, "if you'll climb into your bottle again,
we'll get under way."

Mardak disappeared into the brass bottle with a whishing noise, and Ali, after tucking the bottle securely inside his robe, mounted the camel and started off to meet his destiny.

Destiny met Ali halfway.

He had traveled many miles toward the East when suddenly, against the horizon lit by sunrise, he beheld a small group of horsemen approaching. Eagerly he drove his camel on. He welcomed the breaking of the desert loneliness and he wanted information about his route.

But when at last the riders reached him and surrounded him, his eagerness faded at the sight of their eight leering bearded faces and their eight drawn scimitars.

"By Allah!" said the tallest and ugliest of them, who appeared to be their leader. "Our greetings to thee, rich man's son. What a fortunate chance is ours to be allowed to bask in the radiance of thy gaze."

His companions laughed, and Ali's eyes were dazzled as the sunlight smote their blades.

"Allah's mercy be with thee," said Ali politely. "Although I am not what you think, but only a poor fisherboy, my greeting to you is no less friendly."

The men laughed again, this time even more unpleasantly, and their leader gave a slight and mocking bow.

"Fisherboy!" he cried. "One would not have expected to meet a person of your calling so far from the sea, but now I perceive you speak the truth, indeed, for you have caught many jeweled fish and are bearing them on your hands."

Ali stole a quick and nervous glance at the rings that glistened on his fingers, and wished that he had not been quite so anxious to look like a prince.

"If, of your courtesy," said Ali, "you will direct me toward the city of Baghdad, I will gladly reward you with all the jewelry I possess."

"And if, of our courtesy," said the leader, "we do not direct you on your way to Baghdad, but take you with us and hold you for ransom, your rich father will gladly reward us with all the wealth *he* possesses. Ho! my comrades!" he called to his men. "This is a lucky night! In two short hours we have caught two fine birds . . . the Grand Vizier's daughter and the son of a prince!"

"You do me too great an honor," said Ali. "I am the son neither of a prince nor of a rich man. I am an orphan."

"So much the worse for you!" observed the bandit chief. "For since you have seen us and heard us confess that we have abducted the daughter of the Grand Vizier, we cannot allow you to live to betray us."

And he raised his scimitar high, waving it above his head and showing his teeth in a fierce smile.

Ali, meanwhile, had contrived to remove the cap from his precious bottle, and was desperately trying to think what wish would rescue him completely, and not only halfway, from his plight. Raising his voice, he called out in a solemn tone that froze the bandits in their tracks:

"O thou huge and horrendous Mardak, mightiest of the jinn sealed by Suleiman, and sworn slave of him who hath released you from your captivity, hear my commands and obey! Exercise thy most fearful enchantment, and transform these wicked thieves into a flock of timid sheep!"

The bandit leader, with a scornful look at his men, cried:

"Are ye sheep indeed, that ye stand here stricken by the windy words of a boy? Strike him down! . . . What? Still afeared? Bah! Then I must be the first to . . . baaaaaaaaaa!"

Where the man and the horse had stood, a sheep stood now, and his bleatings were answered by the frightened bleatings of three of his companions, who had also fallen victims to Mardak's enchantment. The four other bandits, with a great shout of fear, spurred their steeds and galloped away as though ten thousand desert devils were on their heels.

Ali drew a deep breath of relief. His glance fell suddenly on a large sack that lay on the sands near by. Something moved within it, and Ali, remembering the bandit's boastful confession, leaped from his camel. He hurried to the sack, drawing his sword as he went. With a quick thrust, he slit the top of the sack and opened it.

Inside, weary and frightened, but more beautiful than the morning star, was the daughter of the Grand Vizier.

Achmed the Lucky, Achmed the Robber Uncle, while he could neither read nor write, was good at arithmetic. He subtracted money from his victims, he divided the loot among his crew, his wicked deeds multiplied. And now, when the bazaars buzzed with the stories of a handsome stranger youth, who dressed in the raiment of a prince but claimed to be only a poor fisherboy, and who had routed a band of dangerous outlaws and rescued the Grand Vizier's daughter, Achmed added two and two and decided that Ali was the answer.

The Grand Vizier had been so overjoyed at the return of his precious daughter that he had rewarded her deliverer with a palace and much gold, and the Caliph himself had heaped honors and titles upon the youth.

Achmed, listening to these things, and remembering how simple and unsuspecting his nephew had been, smiled a secret smile in his beard, and made his plans.

Ali's dreams had come true, or, at any rate, more than halfway true. He was not a prince, but he was a friend of princes. He had not married a princess, but he was betrothed to the Grand Vizier's daughter, who was prettier than any princess he had ever seen or could ever imagine. He lived in a palace, he wore robes of gold and scarlet, he dined off gold and silver plates, he had a chorus of minstrels to entertain him.

And then, one evening, another dream came true.

A servant brought word that a beggar was whining for bread in the courtyard below. Ali went to a balcony, and looked down. The beggar looked up. Despite his shabbiness, his tattered garb and dirty face, he was recognizable as Achmed the Formerly-Lucky.

Ali himself went down to greet the wretched man.

"Can it be?" Achmed cried. "Can it be that I see before me the face of my beloved nephew, Ali, son of my dearest brother? Verily are the words true: The changes of the world are beyond the understanding of men; the proud shall fall and the humble be exalted!"

And he bowed until his forehead touched the ground. Ali, although he pitied the poor man, could not but reflect that never before had Achmed given any signs of considering his nephew "beloved."

"You are welcome to my house, Uncle," he said. "Come. I shall order clothes befitting your years and your wisdom, and then you will join me at table."

Hours later, Achmed, having feasted to his great content, garbed in richer velvets and silks than ever before in his life, was shown by his nephew to luxurious sleeping quarters. With a great exchange of compliments, and ardent wishes that each might have a pleasant and undisturbed sleep, the young man and his wily guest parted.

Achmed slipped into his bed, but he had no intention of sleeping. He waited until the palace was still, and then he stole quietly out of his room and down the stairs, looking for the place in which Ali kept the bulk of his treasures.

His stealthy steps whispered into one chamber after another, and then halted outside an almost closed door that led to a room from which a thin ray of torchlight streamed. He heard Ali's voice, and bent his sharp ear to listen.

"A hundred gold crowns!" Ali was saying. "Oh, Mardak, my servant, I wish a hundred gold crowns!"

A pause . . . then Achmed heard the rattle and the clink-clank-clink of coins pouring onto a stone floor. His curiosity overcoming his caution, Achmed boldly pushed open the door and strode into the room.

Ali looked up in surprise.

"Is something wrong, my uncle?" he asked. "Was your sleep broken by some alarm?"

"Nay," said Achmed cheerfully, "I did not sleep. I could not sleep for thinking of your gracious welcome to me, and I needs must find you to offer thanks again."

The explanation was hard to believe, and Ali did not believe it. He noticed that his uncle's gaze rested hungrily on the pile of gold in the center of the floor, and on the brass bottle beside it. However, before Ali had time to pick up the bottle, Achmed had stepped forward quickly and picked it up himself.

"How strange," exclaimed Achmed, "to find amid such priceless treasures this piece of shabby brassware! In my own poor establishment, this bottle might well feel at home. As a token of the hospitality you have showered upon me here in Baghdad, allow me, I pray, to rid your palace of this trash."

"I would be ashamed," said Ali, "to offer you so poor a thing. Take instead this golden box with seven golden rings."

Achmed waved his hand in protest.

"Your kindness overwhelms me!" he replied. "I do not wish to rob you of. . . ." He decided that the word was not a well-chosen one, and changed it: "I do not wish to deprive you of aught that is of value."

He had removed the bottle's cap, and grinned as the smoke poured out.

"Or is this of some value?" he added, in a harsher voice. "Is this so poor a thing? Perhaps it has within it something of more value than all that is within this palace. . . . Ah! I see now in what fashion your good fortune has come to you! And now it comes to me!"

"You are too hasty, Uncle," said Ali. "The jinni is my servant, not yours."

"We shall see!" said Achmed. He looked down at tiny Mardak, who hovered over the bottle-mouth casting unhappy glances at the two men. "A silly little jinni it is, but a jinni for all that, and my slave! Is it not so, you? Are you not bound to serve the man who releases you from your bottle, and did I not release you these few moments past?"

Mardak glared at the wicked Achmed and gnashed his teeth.

"Answer!" shouted Achmed. "Answer, I charge thee by the name of Suleiman the King!"

Mardak, small as he was, appeared to shrink still more at the mention of this mighty name.

"Alas!" he said, looking helplessly at his young friend Ali. "He speaks the truth. While he has the bottle in his possession, I am obliged to obey him!"

"Good," said Achmed. "Then here is my first command to you. Strike this foolish simpleton of a nephew dead at my feet!"

Mardak groaned, and closed his eyes. A tear splashed into the bottle.

Ali clutched at his heart and fell.

The laughter of Achmed the Lucky rang in chilling

echoes against the stony walls and floor. It rang through the winding halls of the palace. It rang in the cold moonlit courtyard. It rang in the empty streets and alleys of the ancient city as he scurried along them, like a fox making for its hole.

The Tavern of the Eagle's Feather was a dirty, disreputable inn near Baghdad's northern gate, a rendezvous for rascals of all kinds.

Here, as the sun rose over the city walls, Achmed the Lucky crouched in a dingy little room, rubbing his hands in gleeful anticipation. The brass bottle stood on the floor in front of him. Never before in his life had he been so sure that he deserved the name "the Lucky." What luck this has been! Of course, thought Achmed, luck had not played any greater part in this whole affair than his own sharp wits. No! Achmed the Lucky, perhaps, but Achmed the Clever, most certainly!

And now he must display his cleverness in framing a wish for the jinni to bring true. What should he ask for? Money? Millions and millions of golden crowns, to make him the richest man in the kingdom? Or should it be land and palaces?

Achmed, considering these things, found them good, but in the end discarded them. These he would demand later, and they would come to him. But his decision had been made.

The fame of Haroun-al-Raschid, Caliph of Baghdad, resounded throughout the world. No power was as great as his, no name so loved and feared.

Achmed opened the bottle. The smoke drifted. Mardak appeared. He glared at Achmed gloomily.

"What is thy will, O master?" he asked.

"Hear my words and obey!" said Achmed carefully. "That the Caliph of Baghdad be destroyed, and that I, Achmed the Clever, be raised to the highest place in the land!"

Mardak closed his eyes and clapped his hands. For the first time since he had come into Achmed's possession, a dreamy little smile appeared on his lips.

The door of the room was thrust violently open, and a dozen officers fell upon Achmed, shouting:

"Here is the robber we have sought these many months! Away with him to prison!"

Now, O noble hearers young and old, you know, as Achmed did not, that Mardak's power was confined to the granting of but half a wish. The tiny jinni, taking the bandit's commands as representing one wish only, chose to bring to pass only the last half of that wish.

On the following day, Achmed . . . the Unlucky . . . was raised to the highest place in the land . . . a gallows on a steep hill outside the city.

With the passing of Achmed, Mardak was free to return to the young master he loved. For Ali, as you will have guessed, was not dead at all, but only half-dead, and was soon restored to health by the Caliph's own physicians.

The news of Ali's recovery was so pleasing to Haroun that he ordered a half-holiday, and made Ali governor of half a province.

Ali married the Grand Vizier's daughter, and they had six fine children . . . half of them boys, half of them girls.

And they all lived happily, not half-happily, not half-after, but ever after.

And the moral is: Half a jinni is better than none.

The King of the Hares

by ROSALIE K. FRY

PRINCESS Starlight was a very beautiful hare. She belonged to a little girl called Susan, who kept her in a hutch at the back of the moorland cottage where she lived.

Susan was a romantic little girl, and having chosen the most beautiful name she could think of for her pet, she tried to make her life as princess-like as possible. She kept the hutch spotlessly clean, and she drew a crown over the doorway to show that it was the home of royalty. Then, feeling that Starlight would like to hear about other princesses, she brought out her books of fairy tales and read some of the stories aloud to her.

Several of these stories told of princes and princesses bewitched by spells which turned them into birds and animals. Before long Susan began to believe that Princess

[29]

Starlight was under a spell herself, compelled to live in the shape of a hare, when really she was a fairy princess who should live in a palace instead of a hutch. She decided that this was the reason why Starlight never took any notice of her but sat staring out of her hutch with a faraway look in her eyes.

Susan tried everything that the fairy books suggested in the hope of breaking the spell, but nothing made any difference; the Princess went on nibbling cabbage leaves as though she had never eaten off a golden plate in her life.

One night Susan woke to find a flood of moonlight streaming across her bed. She sat up quickly.

Surely this is just the enchanted kind of night when I might see her Royal Highness in her human shape! she thought. She jumped out of bed and hurried downstairs and out into the moonlight. She crept around to the back of the cottage, but although she made no sound, the Princess was there in her hutch as usual, looking as though she had never been anything else but a hare.

Susan wandered away disappointedly, but as she turned to go indoors a wild hare dashed by. She watched him run across the moor, and as he vanished in the distance two more appeared and went frisking after the first. This was too much for Susan's curiosity; she set off across the moor herself in the direction taken by the hares.

She soon found herself on a low hill crowned by a hawthorn tree, from where she looked down into a little hollow. Here she saw a strange scene. Dozens of hares were gathered together, all leaping and dancing in the strangest fashion, some of them stopping from time to time to sit up and box one another with their front paws. Susan watched, fascinated.

Then quite suddenly, for no reason that she could see, they all took fright and left their games in a panic, racing away with frightened eyes, their long ears laid flat.

Susan watched them scatter over the moor and then turned back to the hollow to see what had frightened them. And there to her astonishment stood a tall, brown-haired boy. He was so richly dressed that she guessed at once that he must be a prince or a king.

"Why, hullo!" he said when he saw her. "Have you been there all the time?"

"I was here while the hares were dancing," answered Susan, "but I never saw you among them."

To her surprise the boy looked sad as he replied:

"I expect you did see me dancing with the others. For I am really a hare myself, only I am under a cruel spell and must take this dreadful human shape for a while every night."

This was a new idea to Susan. She knew all about princes being turned into animals, but she had never before heard of an animal being turned into a prince. And this boy did not seem to like his human shape any more than the fairy-tale princes liked their animal ones.

"How did you come to be bewitched?" she asked. "And isn't there a way to break the spell? There usually is in the fairy tales."

"Well, it all happened long ago when I was very young," said the boy, who seemed glad to have someone to talk to. "I was playing alone in the woods when I happened to cross the path of the Elfin King. Unluckily, he took an instant fancy to me, for we hares have always been favorites with the Little People: they know that we have a touch of magic in us and they like to keep us as pets.

"However, I had to explain to His Majesty that I could not be spared to wait on him as he wished, for my father was King of the Hares at that time, and as his eldest son

I had, of course, many duties of my own. But the Elfin King was so furious that he bounded on me shouting:

" 'Very well, if you won't make the best of a good offer you may make the worst of a bad one! From now on you shall spend a part of every night in the shape of your greatest enemy, a human boy!'

"All that was long ago. But although I am now grown up and have become King of the Hares myself, the spell is as strong as ever, and I still find myself in the shape of a human boy for a part of every night."

"And how about breaking the spell, for there surely must be a way?" asked Susan.

"Oh yes, there's a way, all right," replied the boy. "But His Elfin Majesty saw to it that the spell was not likely to be broken ever. For he said it would only be broken when one of my own kind, a hare like myself, would come to me of its own free will and allow me to stroke it while in my human shape.

"But you have seen for yourself what happens. Even my own people run away the instant they see me like this. And yet I have told them about it many times and begged them to stay and break the spell. But as soon as it comes over me and they see this monster shape they forget who I really am, and away they fly in terror." He sighed as he finished his story.

"It isn't really a monster shape, you know," said Susan quickly. "And I know a hare who would not be afraid. For my own Princess Starlight is used to humans, and I am sure she would go to you gladly and even let you pick her up if you wished it."

"Where is she? Oh, please bring her here!" cried the boy eagerly. And then his expression changed.

"But it's too late tonight," he said. "I can feel the change coming over me already. But bring her here to-morrow night—promise, oh, please promise to bring her."

"I promise," said Susan, "and I'll—" She never finished her sentence, for as she spoke the boy disappeared and no one was left but a wild brown hare, who looked at her with startled eyes before darting out of sight.

Princess Starlight was a little surprised when she was lifted out of her hutch the next night, and even more surprised when Susan turned away from the cottage and carried her out on to the moor. As they went, Susan explained to Starlight what she must do:

"And I do so hope you are really able to understand what a wonderful night this is for you," she finished.

William Pène du Bois

"Tonight you are going to be the one to break a spell that has been cast over a king!"

When they reached the hollow the hares were already there, leaping around in their fantastic dance. Susan crouched in the long grass and waited with Starlight in her arms. Presently came the moment she was waiting for, when the hares flew away in panic. Susan stepped out into the open and there stood the young king. He came forward with a smile of welcome.

"Oh, what a beautiful hare!" he exclaimed when he saw the Princess. "If she really breaks the spell may I take her home to my kingdom and make her Queen of the Hares?"

"Oh, I couldn't spare her!" cried Susan, clutching the Princess tightly. But as she spoke she felt a quiver run through the hare in her arms. So the Princess wanted to go!

Susan stood for a moment, thinking it over. After all, hadn't she always wanted to turn Starlight into a real human princess? And if such a thing had happened she could not have expected her to go on living in a hutch at the back of the cottage. She would certainly have married a prince and gone away to live in a castle happily ever after. So would this be any worse, after all? She was not a human princess of course, but here was a real live king wanting to make her Queen of his kingdom.

Princess Starlight quivered again and Susan made up her mind.

"Of course I must let you go and be Queen!" she said gently, and kneeling down, she opened her arms wide.

The Princess bounded across the grass to the King's outstretched hand. As she touched him he vanished and in his place stood a fine brown hare. For a moment he stood there, gazing at Princess Starlight, and then with a flick of their heels they darted away together over the moonlit moor. As they disappeared, Susan thought she heard the young King's voice calling from far away: "Come back when you hear the harebells ring!"

But thinking it over on the way home, she decided she must have imagined it, for who ever heard a harebell make a sound?

Susan missed the Princess very badly, and even the thought of her reigning as Queen didn't quite make up for the empty hutch which still stood in its place behind the cottage.

One night many weeks later, Susan was wakened by a soft chime of bells. She sat up in bed, but even as she did so the sound faded away like the echo of a dream. And yet she knew it was not a dream but something she had really heard. But what bells could be ringing up here on the moor? Suddenly she remembered those half-forgotten words:

"Come back when you hear the harebells ring!"

She was out of bed in a moment, and although there was no further sound of bells she hurried confidently over the moor toward the well-remembered hollow. There was only a crescent moon tonight and the light was dim as she went down into the hollow. There were no hares dancing there, but she half-thought she saw two swift shapes bound off into the shadows.

In the center of the hollow where the grass had been smooth and short, something glimmered palely. She knelt down to see more clearly and found a clump of delicate harebells growing there. They quivered as she bent toward them and she saw a small furry shape crouching among the flowers.

"Oh—oh—it's a baby hare!" she exclaimed. At the sound of her voice the little creature jumped into her lap, where it sat looking up at her with large trustful eyes.

"You little darling, I believe you want to make

friends!" she said as the baby continued to sit in her lap, showing no sign of fear.

And then she guessed what had happened. The King of the Hares and Queen Starlight had left one of their own baby princesses here for her to look after. So those harebell peals *had* been for her after all!

"I shall call you Princess Harebell," said Susan happily as she went home over the moor with the baby clasped in her arms.

William Pène du Bois

The Lost Half-Hour

by HENRY BESTON

ONCE upon a time there was an old widow woman who had three sons. The first two were clever enough but the third, Bobo by name, was little better than a silly. All his mother's scoldings, protests, warnings, and shakings by the collar did him no good whatever.

Now it came to pass that one morning the Princess Zenza, the ruler of the country, happened to pass by the cottage and heard Bobo being given the scolding of all scoldings. Curious as to the cause of all this bother, the Princess drew rein, and summoned Bobo's mother to draw near. On hearing her story, and taking a look at poor, simple Bobo, it occurred to the Princess that so silly a lad might amuse her; so she gave the mother a golden florin, and took Bobo away with her to be her page.

You may be sure that it did not take the wise folk of the castle long to discover how simple a simpleton had arrived. Courtiers, footmen, lackeys, turnspits even, were forever sending him off on ridiculous errands. Now he would be sent to find a white crow's feather or a spray of yellow bluebells; now he was ordered to look for a square wheel or a glass of dry water.

Everybody laughed at him and made fun of him—that is, everybody except little Tilda, the kitchenmaid. When poor Bobo used to return from some wild-goose chase, tired out, mudstained, and often enough wet to the skin, little Tilda, instead of laughing, would find him a glass of warm milk, hang his coat by the fire to dry, and tell him not to be such a simpleton again. Thus, after a while, Bobo learned to ask Tilda's advice before going away on a wild-goose chase, and was in this way saved from many a jest.

Tilda, the kitchenmaid, was as sweet and pretty as she was kind and good. She was said to be the daughter of a beggar woman who had come to the castle one day, asking for help.

On a pleasant midsummer morning, when Bobo had been nearly a year at the castle, Princess Zenza overslept half an hour and did not come down to breakfast at the usual time. When she did rise, she found her court waiting for her in the castle gardens. As she came down the steps of the garden terrace, the Princess looked up at the castle clock to see how late she was, and said to her lady in waiting, "Dear me! Why, I've lost half an hour this morning!"

At these words, Bobo, who was in attendance, pricked up his ears and said, "Please, Your Highness, perhaps I can find it."

At this idea of finding a lost half-hour, the Princess laughed, and found herself echoed by the company.

"Shall we send Bobo in search of the lost half-hour?" said the Princess to the courtiers.

"Yes! Yes!" cried the courtiers. "Bobo shall look for the lost half-hour."

"I'll give him a horse," said one. "I'll give him my old hat," said another. "He can have an old sword I broke last week," said still another.

And so, in less time than it takes to tell about it, poor simpleton Bobo was made ready for his journey.

Before he left the castle, Bobo went down to the kitchen to say good-by to Tilda.

"What, off again?" said the little kitchenmaid. "Where are you going now?"

"The Princess has lost a half-hour and I am going in search of it," said Bobo, proudly. And he told how the Princess herself had commanded him to seek the half-hour through the world, and promised to bring Tilda a splendid present when he returned.

The good kitchenmaid said little, for she feared lest some misadventure overtake the poor simpleton. But when the chief cook was not looking, she tucked a fresh currant bun into Bobo's pocket, and wished him the best of good fortune.

So Bobo went to the castle gate, and mounted his horse, which stumbled and was blind in one eye.

"Good-by, Bobo," cried the assembled courtiers, who were almost beside themselves with laughter. "Don't fail to bring back the lost half-hour!"

So Bobo rode over the hills and far away. Every now and then he would stop a passer-by and ask him if he had seen a lost half-hour.

The first person whom he thus questioned was an old man who was wandering down the road that leads from the Kingdom of the East to the Kingdom of the West.

The Lost Half-Hour

"A lost half-hour?" said the old man. "I've lost something much more serious, I've lost my reputation. You haven't seen a lost reputation lying about here, have you? It was very dignified and wore tortoise-shell glasses."

But Bobo had to answer "No," and the old man wandered on again.

Another day the simpleton encountered a tall, dark, fierce kind of fellow, who answered his polite question with a scream of rage.

"A half-hour," he roared. "No, I haven't seen your half-hour. I wouldn't tell you if I had. What's more, I don't want to see it. I'm looking for something I've lost myself. I've lost my temper. I lost it two years ago at home, and haven't been able to find it anywhere since. Answer me, you silly, have you seen a lost temper anywhere? It's about the size of a large melon and has sharp little points."

On Bobo's answering "No," this dreadful person uttered so perfectly awful a screech of rage that Bobo's horse took fright and ran away with him, and it was all that Bobo could do to rein him in three miles farther down the road.

Still farther along, Bobo came to Ripplebright, the capital city of the Kingdom of the Seven Brooks.

[45]

He was taken before the King himself.

"A lost half-hour?" said the King. "No, I am quite sure it has not been seen in my dominions. Would you mind asking, as you go through the world, for news of my little daughter?" (Here the poor old King took out a great green handkerchief and wiped his eyes.) "She was stolen by the fairies one midsummer eve fifteen years ago. Find her, worthy Bobo, and an immense reward will be yours."

So Bobo left the proud city of Ripplebright, and once again rode over the hills and far away. But never a sign of the lost half-hour did he find, although he asked thousands of people. His faithful white horse died, and he continued his way on foot.

Three long years passed, and Bobo grew into a handsome lad, but remained a simpleton still. Finally, after he had wandered all about Fairyland, he came to the edge of the sea. Finding a ship moored in a little harbor, Bobo asked the sailors if they had seen a lost half-hour.

"No," said the sailors, "but we are going to the Isles of Iron. Suppose you go with us. The lost half-hour may be there."

So Bobo went aboard the ship, and sailed out upon the dark sea.

For two days the weather was warm and clear, but on the third day, there came a dreadful storm, and on the third night the vessel was driven far off her course into the unknown ocean, and was wrecked upon a mysterious isle. A great wave swept the decks, and Bobo was borne away from his companions and carried toward the shining land. Though pounded and battered by the foaming waves, the simpleton at length managed to reach the beach, and took refuge in a crevice of the cliff during the stormy night.

When the dawn broke, all sign of the ship had disappeared. Looking about, Bobo found himself on a lonely island whose heart was a high mountain mass hidden in the fog still sweeping in from the sea. There was not a house, a road, or a path to be seen. Suddenly Bobo noticed a strange little door in the back of a great lonely tree, and, opening this door, he discovered a little cupboard in which was a pair of wooden shoes. Above the shoes was a card, saying simply—

PUT US ON

So Bobo sat down on a stone by the foot of the tree, and put on the wooden shoes, which fitted him very nicely. Now these shoes were magic shoes, and Bobo had hardly

stepped into them before they turned his feet inland. Bobo
obediently let the shoes guide him. At corners the shoes
always turned in the right direction, and if Bobo forgot
and blundered on the wrong way, the shoes swiftly began
to pinch his toes.

For two days Bobo walked inland toward the great
mountain. A warm wind blew the clouds and rain away;
the sun shone sweet and clear. On the morning of the

third day, the simpleton entered a wood of tall, silent trees, and as that day was drawing to a close, the turrets of a magnificent castle rose far away over the leaves of the forest.

Arriving at twilight, Bobo found himself in a beautiful garden lying between the castle walls and the rising slopes of a great mountain. Strange to say, not a living creature was to be seen, and though there were lights in the castle, there was not even a warder at the gate. Suddenly a great booming bell struck seven o'clock; Bobo began to hear voices and sounds. And then, before the humming of the bell had died away, a youth mounted on a splendid black horse dashed at lightning speed out of the castle and disappeared in the wood. An old man with a white beard, accompanied by eleven young men—whom Bobo judged, from their expressions, to be brothers—stood by the gate to see the horseman ride away.

Plucking up courage, Bobo came forward, fell on his knee before the old man, and told his story.

"Truly, you should thank the storm fairies," said the old man; "for had you not been wrecked upon this island, never would you have discovered the lost half-hour. I am Father Time himself, and these are my twelve sons, the

Hours. Every day, one after the other, they ride for an hour round the whole wide world. Seven O'Clock has just ridden forth. Yes, you shall have the lost half-hour, but you must look after my sons' horses for the space of a whole year."

To this Bobo willingly agreed, and Twelve O'Clock, who was the youngest of the Hours, took him to the stables and showed him the little room in the turret that he was to have. For a year Bobo served Father Time and his sons. He took such good care of the great black horses of the Hours of the Night, and the white horses of the Hours of the Day, that they were never more proud and strong, nor their coats smoother and more gleaming.

When the year was up, Bobo again sought out Father Time.

"You have served faithfully and well," said Father Time. "Here is your reward." And, with these words, he placed in Bobo's hands a small, square casket made of ebony. "The half-hour lies inside. Don't try to peek at it or open the box until the right time has come. If you do, the half-hour will fly away and disappear forever."

"Farewell, Bobo," said kind young Twelve O'Clock,

who had been the simpleton's good friend. "I, too, have a gift for thee. Drink this cup of water to the last drop." And the youth handed the simpleton a silver cup full to the brim of clear shining water.

Now this water was the water of wisdom, and when Bobo had drunk it, he was no longer a simpleton. And being no longer a simpleton, he remembered the man who had lost his reputation, the man who had lost his temper, and the king whose daughter had been stolen by the fairies. So Bobo made so bold as to ask Father Time about them, for Father Time knows everything that has happened in the whole wide world.

"Tell the first," said Father Time, "that his reputation has been broken into a thousand pieces which have been picked up by his neighbors and carried home. If he can persuade his neighbors to give them up, he should be able to piece together a pretty good reputation again. As for the man who lost his temper, tell him that it is to be found in the grass by the roadside close by the spot where you first met him. As for the missing daughter, she is the kitchenmaid in Princess Zenza's palace, who is known as Tilda."

So Bobo thanked Father Time, and at noon, Twelve

O'Clock placed him behind him on the white charger, and hurried away. So fast they flew that Bobo, who was holding the ebony casket close against his heart, was in great danger of falling off. When they got to the seashore, the white horse hesitated not an instant but set foot upon the water, which bore him up as if it had been, not water, but earth itself.

Once arrived at the shore of Fairyland, Twelve O'Clock stopped, wished Bobo good speed, and, rising in the air, disappeared into the glare of the sun. Bobo, with the precious ebony casket in his hand, continued on in the direction of Princess Zenza's palace.

On the second morning of his journey, he happened to see far ahead of him on the highway the unfortunate aged man who had lost his reputation. To him, Bobo repeated the counsel of Father Time, and sent him hurrying home to his neighbors' houses. Of the man who had lost his temper, Bobo found no sign. In the grass by the roadside, however, he did find the lost temper—a queer sort of affair like a melon of fiery red glass all stuck over with uneven spines and brittle thorns. Bobo, with great goodness of heart, took along this extraordinary object, in the hope of finding its angry possessor.

Farther on, the lad encountered Tilda's father, the unhappy King, and delivered his message. The joy of the monarch knew no bounds, and Bobo, the one-time simpleton, became on the spot Lord Bobo of the Sapphire Hills, Marquis of the Mountains of the Moon, Prince of the Valley of Golden Apples, and Lord Seneschal of the proud City of Ripplebright—in a word, the greatest nobleman in all Fairyland. Then, having assembled a magnificent following of great nobles, all in splendid silks, and soldiers in shining armor, the delighted King rode off to claim his missing daughter from Princess Zenza.

On they rode, the harnesses jingling, the bridle bells ringing, and the breastplates of the armed men shining in the sun. After a week of almost constant progress (for the King was so anxious to see his beloved daughter that he would hardly give the cavalcade time to rest), they came to the frontiers of Princess Zenza's kingdom.

Strange to say, black mourning banners hung from the trees, and every door in the first village which the travelers saw was likewise hung with black streamers. On the steps of one of the cottages sat an old woman, all alone and weeping with all her might.

"What *is* the matter, my good woman?" said the King.

"O sir," said the peasant woman, "evil days have fallen upon our unhappy kingdom. Three days ago a terrible dragon alighted in the gardens of the palace and sent word to Princess Zenza that if within three days she did not provide him with someone brave enough to go home with him and cook his meals and keep his cavern tidy, he would burn our fields with his fiery breath. Yet who, I ask you, would be housekeeper for a dragon? Suppose he didn't like the puddings you made for him—why, he might eat you up! All would have been lost had not a brave little kitchenmaid named Tilda voluntered to go. It is for her that we are mourning. At two o'clock she is to be carried off by the dragon. It is almost two now. Alas! Alas!"

Hardly were the words out of her mouth, when the town bell struck twice, solemnly and sadly.

"Quick! quick!" cried the King and Bobo in the same breath; "let us hurry to the castle. We may be able to save her yet."

But they knew in their hearts that they were too late, and that poor Tilda had given herself to the dragon. And so it proved. In spite of his mad dash, Bobo, who had spurred on ahead, arrived exactly half an hour late. The monstrous dragon with Tilda in his claws was just a little smoky speck far down the southern sky. Princess Zenza and all her court stood by weeping and wringing their jeweled hands.

Suddenly Bobo thought of the half-hour. He had arrived half an hour late, *but he could have that half-hour back again!* Things should be exactly as they were half an hour before.

He opened the cover of the ebony box. Something like a winged white flame escaped from it, and flew hissing through the air to the sun. As for the sun itself, turning round like a cartwheel and hissing like ten thousand rockets, it rolled back along the sky to the east. The hands of the clocks, which marked half-past two, whirred back to two o'clock in a twinkling. And, sure enough, there was brave little Tilda standing alone in a great field waiting for the dragon to come and take her away. Lumbering heavily along like a monstrous turtle, and snorting blue smoke, the dragon was advancing toward her.

Bobo ran down into the field and stood beside Tilda, ready to defend her to the end.

The dragon came nearer and nearer. Suddenly, angered by the sight of Bobo and his drawn sword, he roared

angrily, but continued to approach. Bobo struck at him with his sword. The blade broke upon his steely scales. The dragon roared again. Now just as the dragon's mouth was its widest, Bobo, who had been searching his pockets desperately, hurled into it *the lost temper.*

There was a perfectly terrific *bang!* as if a million balloons had blown up all at once. For the dragon was blown to pieces. The lost temper had finished him. Only one fragment of him, a tiny bit of a claw, was ever found.

Everybody, you may be sure, began to cry "Hurrah" and "Hooray," and soon they were firing off cannon and ringing all the bells. Then Tilda's father took her in his arms, and told her that she was a real princess. The Grand Cross of the Order of the Black Cat was conferred upon Bobo by Princess Zenza, who also asked his pardon for having treated him so shabbily. This Bobo gave readily. A wonderful fete was held. When the rejoicings were over, Bobo and Tilda were married, and lived happily together all their days.

The Little Scarred One

Retold by CAROLINE CUNNINGHAM

IN days long ago, a young Indian brave lived with his sister on the border of a lovely lake in the north country. She took care of his lodge, which was the finest one in the whole region. He was tall and handsome and all the Indian girls wished to marry him. He was guarded by a good spirit who had given him a magic arrow, so he caught more game than anyone else.

The spirit also had made it possible for him to be invisible when he wished, to everyone but his sister and the girl who would someday come with the power to see him. This girl, he would know, was the one intended to be his wife.

Toward evening when the sun was low, the Invisible One always returned home from hunting. His canoe came across the water as lightly as a leaf in the breeze. Then his sister would walk down to the shore of the lake with any girl who might have come to the lodge that day in the hope of seeing him.

To his sister he was always visible, and as his canoe approached the shore she would ask: "Do you see my brother?" Sometimes the girls would truthfully answer: "No." Oftener the word would be: "Yes." Then the sister would say: "What is his shoulder strap made of?"

There were only two things the Indians used in making shoulder straps: either a strip of rawhide or a green withe from an ash tree. Sometimes a girl would answer, "It's made of rawhide"; or sometimes, "The withe of an ash tree."

Knowing that her companion who said either of these things had not told the truth, the sister would reply quietly and kindly: "Come, let us return to the wigwam."

Some of the girls would stay to help cook the supper. They would wait with great curiosity to see the hunter eat. There was proof enough that he was a real person, for his moccasins, as he took them off, at once became visible and his sister would put them away.

Beyond this, however, the girls could see nothing,

though many of them remained all night. Try as hard as they could, no one but his sister had ever seen the young brave.

Now, in a village at the extreme end of the lake there lived an old Indian with his three daughters. The mother was dead, so there was no one to see that the youngest girl got her share of everything. The child's bright eyes were sad with care. Often tears ran down her cheeks as she went for water or gathered wood.

She was a timid little thing, though very beautiful. Her sisters were jealous and hated her. They made her stay in a dark corner at the back of the lodge where no one could ever look at her. But she passed her time arranging beads and sewing them on her sisters' clothes in patterns like the flowers of earth and the stars of heaven.

When their father was away on his hunting trips the two elder sisters were very cruel; they abused her in every way they could think of, and made her sweep up all the hot ashes. She was small and weak and often ill, but this did not prevent them from treating her with great unkindness. Finally her body was scarred and her hair was singed, and the people in the village called her the Little Scarred One.

When her father would return and see her burns, he would ask: "How did this happen, my little one?" But she was afraid of her sisters and dared not tell him.

"Oh, it is all her own fault," the eldest sister would say. "We tell her not to go near the fire, but she always disobeys us and plays in the hot ashes. We can't keep her away."

The Little Scarred One was very lonely. She would sit by the lake at night, longing for her mother to come back to her. "I want my mother, I'm so lonesome," she would sob to herself. But her mother never came back.

One day it entered the heads of the two elder sisters to try their luck at seeing the Invisible One. They dressed themselves in their finest clothes, for they wished to look their best.

On reaching the lodge, they found the young brave's sister at home, and at sunset they went with her along the accustomed walk to the water's edge. When her brother approached in his canoe, she asked them if they saw him, and both answered: "Certainly."

They lied like many others. One said the shoulder strap was made of rawhide, and the other said it was an ash withe.

So they, too, had to return to the lodge without seeing him. But they stayed on and on, hoping to catch a glimpse of him while he was eating.

They saw his game drop to the ground at the door. They saw his moccasins after he had taken them off. But when he ate, the food became invisible as soon as he touched it. So the two girls had to go home angry and disappointed.

They were more cruel than ever to the Little Scarred One.

The next morning their father returned, bringing with him a great many pretty shells. The older sisters were soon busy stringing them, and the little girl begged for a few. The eldest refused, but the other one threw her a handful.

The Little Scarred One knew where her sisters had been, and she thought dreamily: "Maybe—maybe I could see him. Then how many things might happen!"

But she had no pretty clothes. She was almost in rags. What could she do?

The poor child had always gone barefoot. So she had to take a pair of her father's moccasins and put them in water to make them smaller and softer and easier to wear.

Nearby, a silver birch stood, dressed in its beautiful white bark, and she thought: "Maybe my mother's spirit has entered the birch tree." For the Indians believed that every created thing had an indwelling spirit. She asked for just enough of the birch tree's covering to make a dress and leggings. She drew some figures on it by scraping and peeling the bark, and then made the dress. In this odd apparel, wearing her father's moccasins and with a few strings of shells wound about her head because she had no beautiful braids, the strange little creature went forth bravely to try her luck.

For even the Little Scarred One wished to see the wondrous hunter in the great wigwam at the other end of the lake.

Her sisters called after her jeeringly: "Come back, come back, you silly little thing!"

As she passed through the village, the children and even the men and women laughed and hooted. Some of them said sadly: "Go back, Little Scarred One. It's no use." But she went on. For she had made a great resolve. Maybe it was the spirit in the birch tree that had inspired her.

When the poor little girl in her clothing of bark, with

hair singed and her face scarred, reached the hunter's lodge, his sister received her most kindly, for she knew more than the mere outside of things as the world knows them.

At sunset the two girls went down to the shore. Off in the distance sounded the faint drip-drip, drip-drip of the brother's canoe paddle. He was coming! They stood shading their eyes from the flush of the sun as they gazed across the lake. At last the sister said, "Do you see him now?"

The Little Scarred One replied with awe, "Yes, truly I do see him. He is wonderful."

"Then tell me what his shoulder strap is made of," the sister asked searchingly.

"It is the Rainbow," she said. And great fear came upon her.

"But what is his bowstring?" asked the young hunter's sister.

"His bowstring is the Milky Way—the bridge of souls," answered the Little Scarred One.

"Truly you have seen him," said his sister. "Now we must go back to the lodge and prepare for his coming."

The two girls hurried home. The sister opened a chest

of treasures in which lay the most beautiful clothes the
Little Scarred One had ever seen, though at thought of
herself she hung her head in sorrow. But the sister bathed
her in magic water and a wonderful thing happened: as

the water touched her, all the scars vanished from her face and body. The sister combed her hair and under the comb it grew long and shining, like a blackbird's wing. Her eyes shone like stars. In all the world there was no such beauty.

The sister dressed the Little Scarred One in a wedding garment and adorned her with precious shells. She placed her in the wife's seat next the door and the two waited.

At last they heard the game drop to the ground outside the lodge. The skins hanging at the doorway were drawn aside and there stood the Invisible One, handsome and wonderful. He smiled down upon the Little Scarred One kindly and said:

"So we have found each other!"

"Yes," she answered, shyly and worshipfully.

In the blue cool of evening, as the sun was setting beneath the edge of the world and the red was turning to black, the Little Scarred One became the wife of the hunter. They were married under a silver birch tree just by speaking a word—as is the Indian custom. The butterflies knew her and fluttered about. Flowers blossomed in the fragrant night air and greeted her with their scentladen murmurs as she passed back into the wigwam.

William Pène du Bois.

The Dreamer

by KATHARINE PYLE

THERE once lived a man and his wife, named Peter and Kate, and they were so poor that they had scarcely enough bread to put in their mouths. They lived in a wretched, miserable hut, and in front of the hut was a river, and back of it a patch of ground and a gnarled old apple tree.

One night when Peter was sleeping he dreamed a dream, and in this dream a tall old man dressed in gray, and with a long gray beard, came to him and said, "Peter, I know that you have had a hard life, and have neither grumbled nor complained, and now I have a mind to help you. Follow down the river until you come to a bridge. On the other side of the river you will see a town. Take up your stand on the bridge and wait there patiently. It may be that nothing will happen the first day, and it may be that nothing will happen the second day either, but if you do not lose courage, but still wait patiently, some time during the third day someone will come to you, and tell you something that will make your fortune for you."

In the morning, when Peter awoke, he told his dream to Kate, his wife. "It would be a curious thing if I should do as the old man told me and really become rich," said he.

"Nonsense!" answered his wife. "Dreams are nothing but foolishness. Do you go over to Neighbor Goodkin and see whether he has not some wood to be cut, so you can earn a few pence to buy meal for tomorrow."

So Peter did as his wife told him, and went over to his neighbor's and worked there all day, and by evening he had almost forgotten his dream.

But that night, as soon as he fell asleep, the old man appeared before him again. "Why have you not done as I told you, Peter?" said he. "Remember, good luck will not wait forever. Tomorrow do you set out for the bridge and town I told you of, and believe, for it is the truth; if you wait there for three days and make the best of what will then be told you, you will become a rich man."

When Peter awoke the next morning, his first thought

was to set out in search of the bridge and town of which the old man had told him, but still his wife dissuaded him.

"Do not be so foolish," said she "Sit down and eat your breakfast and be thankful that you have it. You earned a few pence yesterday, and who knows but what you may be lucky enough to earn even more today."

So Peter did not set out on his journey in search of fortune that day either.

But the next night for the third time the old man appeared before him, and now his look was stern and forbidding. "Thou fool!" said he. "Three times have I come to thee, and now I will come no more. Go to the bridge of which I have spoken and listen well to what is there said to thee. Otherwise want and poverty will still be thy portion, even as they have been heretofore."

With this the old man disappeared, and Peter awoke. And now it was of no use for his wife to scold and argue. As the old man had commanded so Peter would do. He only stopped to put some food in his stomach and more in his pockets, and off he set, one foot before another.

For a long time Peter journeyed on down the river till he was both footsore and weary, and then he came to a bridge that crossed the stream, and on the other side was a town, and Peter felt almost sure this was the place to which the old man of his dreams had told him to come.

So he took his stand on the bridge and stayed there all day. The passers-by stared at him, and some of them spoke to him, but none of them said to him anything that might, by any chance, lead him on to fortune. All that day he waited on the bridge, and all of the day after, and by the time the third day came, he had eaten all the food he had brought with him except one hard, dry crust of bread. Then he began to wonder whether he were not a simpleton to be loitering there day after day, all because of a dream, when he might, perhaps, be earning a few pennies at home in one way or another.

Now just beyond this bridge there was a tailor's shop, and the tailor who lived there was a very curious man. Ever since Peter had taken his stand on the bridge the tailor had been peeping out at him, and wondering why he was standing there, and what his business might be; and the longer Peter stayed the more curious the tailor became. He fussed and he fidgeted, and along toward the afternoon of the third day he could bear it no longer, and he put aside his work and went out to the bridge to find out what he could about Peter and what he was doing there.

When he came where Peter was he bade him good day.

"Good day," answered Peter.

"Are you waiting here on the bridge for someone?" asked the tailor.

"I am and I am not," replied Peter.

"Now what may be the meaning of that?" asked the tailor. "How can you be waiting and still not be waiting all at one and the same time?"

"I am waiting for someone—that is true," said Peter; "but I know not who he is nor whence he will come, nor, for the matter of that, whether anyone will come at all." And then he related to the tailor his dream, and how he had been told that if he waited on the bridge for three days someone would come along and tell him something that would make him rich for life.

"Why, what a silly fellow you are," said the tailor. "I, too, have dreamed dreams, but I have too much sense to pay any attention to them. Only last week I dreamed three times that an old man came to me and told me to follow up along the bank of the river until I came to a hut where a man and his wife lived—the man's name was Peter, and his wife's name was Kate. I was to go and dig among the roots of an apple tree back of this house, and there, buried among the roots of the tree, I would find a chest of golden money. That was what I dreamed. But did I go wandering off in search of such a place? No, indeed, I am not such a simpleton. I stick to my work, and I can manage to keep a warm roof over my head, and have plenty of food to eat, and when I am dressed in my best there is not one of the neighbors that looks half as fine as I do. No, no; go back to where you belong and set to work, my man, and maybe you can earn something better than those miserable rags you are wearing now."

So said the tailor, and then he went back to his tailor's bench and his sewing.

But Peter stood and scratched his head. "A man named Peter, and his wife named Kate! And an apple tree behind the house!" said he. "Now it's a strange thing if a fortune's been lying there under the roots of the apple tree all this while, and I had to come to this town and this bridge to hear about it!"

So said Peter as he stood there on the bridge. But then, after he had scratched his head and thought a bit longer, he pulled his hat down over his ears and off he set for home. The farther he went, the more of a hurry he was in, and at last, when he came within sight of his house again, he was all out of breath with the haste he had made.

He did not wait to go inside, but he bawled to his wife to fetch him a pick and shovel, and ran around the house to where the apple tree stood.

His wife did not know what had happened to him. She thought he must have lost his wits, but she brought him the pick and shovel, and he began digging around about the roots of the apple tree.

He had not dug for so very long when his pick struck something hard. He flung the pick aside and seized his spade, and presently he uncovered a great chest made of stout oak wood and bound about with iron.

The chest was so heavy that he could not lift it out of the hole himself, and his wife had to help him. The chest was locked, but that mattered little to Peter. He took his pick, and with a few blows he broke the hinges and fastenings, and lifted the lid from its place. At once he gave a loud cry, and fell on his knees beside the chest. He and his wife could scarce believe in their good fortune. It was brimming over with golden money, enough to make them rich for life.

They carried the chest into the house, and barred the door, and set about counting the money, and there was so much of it, they were all evening and part of the night counting it.

That was the way good fortune came to Peter, and all by the way of a dream.

Now he and his wife built themselves a great house, and had fine food, and coaches, and horses, and handsome clothes, and they feasted the neighbors, and never a poor man came to the door but what they gave him as much food as he could eat and a piece of silver to put in his pocket.

One day Peter put on his finest clothes and made his wife dress herself in her best, and then they stepped into one of their coaches, and Peter bade the coachman drive to the town where he had stood on the bridge and listened to the tailor tell his dream of the chest of money buried under the apple tree.

Peter made the coachman drive up in front of the tailor's shop, and when the tailor saw the coach stopping at his door, and the fine people sitting in it, he thought it was some great nobleman and his wife, come perhaps to order a suit of clothes of him.

He came out, bowing and smiling and smirking, and Peter said to him, "Do you remember me?"

"No, your lordship," answered the tailor, still bowing and smiling, "I have not that honor, your lordship."

Then Peter told him he was the ragged fellow who had stood out there on the bridge waiting for good luck to come to him; and sure enough it had, for if it had not been for the dream the tailor told him, he would have known nothing about the gold buried under the apple tree and would never have become the rich man he was now.

When the tailor heard this tale, he was ready to tear his hair out, for if he had believed his dream he might have found the gold himself and have kept a share of it.

However, Peter gave him a hundred gold pieces to comfort him and ordered a fine suit. He also promised that after that he would buy all his clothes from the tailor and pay him a good price for them, so the tailor, too, got some good from all the dreaming.

William Pène du Bois

The Trials of Ting Ling

by VERNON BOWEN

A LONG time ago, before your great-grandfather's great-great-grandfather was born, there lived in China a poor juggler's helper called Ting Ling.

The juggler went from town to town giving performances in the streets. He juggled swords and swallowed them. He did tricks of magic.

It was Ting Ling's job to take care of the knives and swords his master juggled. It was his job, too, to do handstands, flip-flops, and cartwheels to entertain the audiences.

It was also his job to dance on a tightrope stretched high over the street.

Now in those days, China was ruled by a cruel, fat man named Wo Ti. Fat men are supposed to be jolly fellows, but the Emperor Wo Ti was not. He was very fat, and he was very cruel. He was feared from the cold and lofty mountains of Tibet to the hot and steaming jungles of Sumatra.

Wo Ti had four great passions in life. He loved to eat. He loved to see men suffer. He loved jade. And he loved his young daughter, the Princess Dar Ling.

The Emperor had great ambitions for his daughter. He dreamed of seeing her grow up to be Empress of all Cathay, and of the lands to the west, and the Islands of Nippon to the east, and perhaps even of the land of India to the south. And, as he sat on the Dragon Throne, he wondered to what prince he might betroth her, so that her marriage might win more lands for her to rule. But as he went over in his mind the princes he knew, he could think of none who was worthy of the Princess Dar Ling's hand.

Wo Ti so treasured his daughter that he could not bear to have anyone else look at her and see how fair she was. In the palace where she lived, even the nobility of the court had to kneel, with heads touching the floor, when she went past. No one but the royal family and the Princess' nurse and governess were permitted to see Dar Ling's face.

The Trials of Ting Ling

As for the common people, they could not even appear in the streets when the curtained palanquin of the Emperor, guarded by a hundred giant, armed slaves, and with the Princess hidden inside, was carried between one of Wo Ti's palaces and another. If a commoner was unlucky enough to be abroad when the palanquin passed, he had to lie flat on the ground and cover his eyes. Otherwise, it was sudden death for him. If he looked up, one of the slaves instantly lopped off his head.

Princess Dar Ling led a lonely life. She had no friends. When she played in the palace garden, she really didn't play at all, for she did not know how to play. She walked sedately among the gorgeous trees and beautiful flowers. She looked at the strange, mulelike deer in the palace park. She watched the imperial goldfish in their pool. But there was little else to do.

As the Princess grew older, the Emperor's ministers begged him to betroth her to some powerful prince. But he delayed and delayed, not wishing to have Dar Ling out of his sight. The ministers humbly but firmly insisted, day after day, and week after week, and month after month, until the Emperor grew so weary of their pleading that he agreed.

But there was a catch to his agreement. He agreed that he would betroth the Princess to any suitor who would slay the Golden Dragon.

At this, the ministers were in despair, for no man could prevail against the Golden Dragon that lived in a cave outside Peking. His scales were like brass. Neither spear nor arrow could pierce them. The dragon had already eaten more good men than they could count.

"Some other task!" the ministers cried.

But Wo Ti would not be moved.

So the ministers sent out a proclamation to all the kingdoms of the world. And many princes, hearing of the beauty of Dar Ling, came to slay the dragon, but all of them left their bones in the monster's cave.

The ministers begged the Emperor to select another task, but he would not. And thus matters stood for some time.

Now, one fine, warm spring day, when the peach blossoms had burst from bud, and the bees had come sleepily from their hives to rob the blossoms of their honey, the juggler and Ting Ling arrived at a small village near one of the Emperor's palaces. They set up their apparatus, stretching the tightrope high over the street. Ting Ling got the swords and knives and gilded balls out of the wheelbarrow, and they started to give a performance.

The juggler swallowed swords and juggled the gilded balls. Ting Ling whirled through cartwheels and flip-flops like a pinwheel.

Then it was time for Ting Ling to dance on the tight-rope.

He took his balancing umbrella and climbed to the rooftop where one end of the rope was anchored. He ran out to the middle of the rope, his feet twinkling. Then, he started to dance.

And at this very moment, a great shout arose from the village street. The Emperor's palanquin was coming! In a flash, the people who had been laughing at Ting Ling's antics on the tightrope disappeared indoors. So did the juggler. And there was Ting Ling standing high over the middle of the street on the tightrope as royalty approached.

There was no time to go anywhere.

Ting Ling thought of running quickly to one of the rooftops and lying down there. But it was too late. The guardsmen had seen him. There was only one thing to do, and he did it. He lay down on the tightrope, closed his eyes, covered them with his hands, and hoped for the best. But this did not satisfy the guards.

"Shoot him down," cried the captain.

Instantly, an archer nocked a razor-sharp broadhead arrow to his bow, hooked his brass thumb ring on the string, and let fly at Ting Ling.

Whhht!

The arrow whizzed up through the air.

But instead of hitting the boy, it hit and severed the stretched tightrope. And Ting Ling, hunched into a ball, turned end over end as a good acrobat should, and hurtled toward the ground.

But he never touched it. Instead, he fell with a crash through the red-lacquered top of the palanquin and landed on some soft cushions. When he opened his eyes, he was looking at the most beautiful girl he had ever seen.

It was the Princess Dar Ling.

Outside the palanquin, the armed slaves were making a terrible outcry. The juggler's helper should be dragged out and killed. But who was going to do the dragging? None of them was permitted to look at the face of the Princess, and he who did so was sure to die. They shouted among themselves for quite a while, and then one of them thought of simply reaching into the palanquin with his hand, without looking in, and dragging the unfortunate Ting Ling out. But when he thrust his arm between the curtains, the Princess, who hadn't seen anything so exciting in all her life, said, "Let him alone, or I shall have all of your heads chopped off."

So the miserable slaves, not knowing what else to do, picked up the palanquin and carried the Princess and Ting Ling to the palace. When they got there, they set the palanquin down in the courtyard and threw themselves on their faces while Dar Ling, followed by Ting Ling, got out of the palanquin and walked into the Emperor's great audience chamber.

Wo Ti's face first turned bright turkey red, and then purple, when he saw the juggler's helper.

"Who is that?" he shouted, pointing one of his gold-cased fingernails at Ting Ling, who promptly threw himself face down on the floor.

"That," said the Emperor's daughter, "is Ting Ling. He is a boy. I have never talked to a boy before. He is very interesting."

"He has committed sacrilege by even seeing your face,"

thundered the Emperor, "let alone talking to you, let alone riding in the palanquin with you; and he shall die for it! I shall have his head lopped from his shoulders instantly!"

And the Emperor picked up a golden hammer to strike a gong and summon a slave.

But the Princess was not her father's daughter for nothing.

"No," she cried, and she stamped her foot.

The Emperor was taken aback. Nobody had ever contradicted him before.

"I like this boy very much," said the Princess. "Maybe I would like to marry *him*."

"But he is not a prince," roared the Emperor. "He is only a beggar boy."

"Ah, but he is very clever," said the Princess. "Perhaps he can succeed where all the others have failed. And if he is to die, at least give him his chance. Let him fight the Golden Dragon."

The Emperor smiled wickedly. "Very well, let him meet the dragon," he said.

Poor Ting Ling! He was going from the frying pan into the fire.

But he was not discouraged.

"Let me have a spear and a sword, and I shall fight your dragon," he said.

So the next morning, a sword and spear were brought to Ting Ling and he, followed by a huge crowd that stayed at a respectful distance behind him, started out boldly to meet the dragon.

The Emperor went along, too. He rode in a silken palanquin carried by fifty slaves, and beside him sat Dar Ling, her face veiled so that none could see her. It was a magnificent procession, with ragged Ting Ling trudging along far ahead of it and the common people throwing themselves on their faces as the royal party followed him.

When he got near the cave where the dragon lived, Ting Ling sat down on a rock to think things over. He knew that his sword and spear, even though very sharp, could not pierce the tough scales of the dragon. But what could he do?

Presently, he had an idea. He grasped the spear in his left hand, the sword in his right, and ran toward the cave, shouting to the dragon to come out.

Hissing like a steam engine, the dragon slithered out of the cave and rushed toward Ting Ling, its great red mouth wide open.

And Ting Ling stepped right into the dragon's mouth!
The Princess let out a little wail of anguish. The Emperor smiled evilly. That was the end of the fellow, he thought.

But it wasn't. For as Ting Ling stepped into the dragon's mouth, he held his long spear upright, and when the dragon tried to snap his jaws together, he couldn't because the spear was wedged between those jaws, propping them wide open.

Ting Ling had decided to fight the dragon from the *inside* rather than the outside. And now he cut and hacked and thrust inside the dragon until the big beast was as dead as a doornail. Then Ting Ling strolled out of the dragon's mouth.

A great cheer arose from the crowd. The Princess Dar Ling smiled. The Emperor Wo Ti scowled.

"Ah," said the Emperor's ministers, "now betroth him to the Princess."

"No," said the Emperor. "He is only a worthless juggler. And killing the dragon was easy. Let him try another task. Let him try to raise the sunken bronze bell of Lotus Pool."

The ministers were silent. The Princess Dar Ling sighed. Trying to raise the great bell had taken the lives of men for generations. The bell, which weighed a solid ten tons, had been toppled from its tower and into the crystal-clear waters of Lotus Pool by an invading army full five centuries before Ting Ling was born. It lay forty feet deep, and the best engineers of ten succeeding emperors had not succeeded in raising it. How then could a mere boy succeed where so many gifted men had failed?

But Ting Ling took the news without getting excited. "Take me to see this bell," he said calmly.

So they took him to see the bell, half-sunk in the mud and grasses at the bottom of Lotus Pool. Ting Ling looked at it and then sat down on a stone bench at the side of the pool to think things over. For a long, long time he sat still, thinking, while all the court waited. Then he had an idea!

"Bring me ten bullock cartloads of short lengths of bamboo," he said finally. "And a cartload of stout cord."

The crowd wondered at this request, but the things he wanted were brought to Ting Ling. When they arrived, Ting Ling shed most of his clothes, took one of the short lengths of bamboo and tied one end of a long cord to it. Then he dove into the water and swam down to the bell. He passed the end of the cord through the bronze loop on top of the bell, dragged the hollow bamboo section that was full of air down close to the bell, tied it fast, and then shot up to the surface.

He did the same thing with another cord and another piece of bamboo. And another and another and another until, finally, he had fastened hundreds of hollow, buoyant sections of bamboo to the great bell. At last, the upward pull exerted by all the air in those bamboo sections heaved the bell from its muddy bed and it shot to the surface, with Ting Ling bobbing beside it.

Great cheers burst from the crowd. The Princess Dar Ling laughed delightedly. But the Emperor scowled.

"Too easy. Too easy," he said. "Let him try something hard. Let him get rid of the Mongolian Giant."

At this, a great sigh arose from the ministers, for the Mongolian Giant was the most fearsome giant in all the world. He was as tall as a pine tree. With one sweep of his great sword, he could mow down whole armies.

But Ting Ling was not frightened. "Show me this giant," he said calmly.

So they took him on a long journey to the gorge of the mighty Hwang Ho River, where the Mongolian Giant lay in wait to wreck and rob the river boats. When they got near, Ting Ling sat down on a log to think about the problem. He thought a long time, and finally he said, "I should like to have a cork."

A cork. Just a cork. No spears. No swords. No slings. No bows and arrows. He was going to fight a giant with a cork? How could he do that? The courtiers looked dumfounded, but somebody pulled a cork from a water bottle and gave it to Ting Ling, and he started forth. All the others stayed at a safe distance from him.

As Ting Ling walked toward the gorge, he kept looking up into the trees along the way. Presently he spied what he wanted and, creeping up softly toward something that looked like a large pudding, he pushed the cork into it and broke off the twig on which the object was hanging. Then, carrying it easily in one hand, he shouted to the giant to come out and fight.

With an echoing bellow, the giant rushed out of his cave, whirling his terrible sword above his head. Ting Ling stood his ground until the giant was nearly upon him. Then he flung the object he had been carrying at the giant's feet, right under the monster's billowing robe. And then he whirled and ran away.

The giant roared as the hornets in the nest that Ting Ling smashed on the ground began to sting him. They stung his hands. They stung his arms and legs and face. He was blinded. He was furious! Howling with rage and

pain, he followed the sound of Ting Ling's footsteps, running toward the river. Swiftly, the giant tore after the fleeing boy.

At the cliff's edge, Ting Ling turned sharply to one side and stood still while the giant rushed onward, onward, onward—over the brink of the cliff and into the roaring river where he was lost forever.

"Now betroth the juggler to the Princess!" cried the Emperor's ministers. But Wo Ti still refused. For now he was afraid of Ting Ling. Anyone so clever would not let the Emperor Wo Ti remain Emperor long. So the wily Wo Ti proposed one last test.

"If he is so clever," he cried, "let him make a fire with *water*. If he succeeds, he shall be betrothed to the Princess. If he fails—he shall lose his head."

Ting Ling sat down on the grass to think about the problem.

Who ever heard of making a fire with water?

The Emperor gloated, feeling sure he was rid of this clever juggler boy at last! But the Princess, behind her curtains in the palanquin, smiled hopefully.

Ting Ling stared at the grass at his feet. He saw a single drop of dew glistening in the center of a broad leaf.

He had an idea. In his travels, he had seen many things, and he remembered the burning lenses he had seen used by a wandering magician.

He plucked a blade of grass and knotted one end into a loop. He caught the single drop of water in the loop, frayed some fluffy cotton from the edge of his old robe, and then held the drop of water between the sun and the cotton lint. The drop of water was a perfect, round lens. As the sun's rays focused through it, the lint began to smoke a little and then burst into flame. Ting Ling had made a fire with water!

The ministers and courtiers shouted in amazement. The Princess laughed.

And Wo Ti? He was so furiously, red-faced angry that he suffered a stroke of apoplexy and perished on the spot.

So the ministers proclaimed Ting Ling Emperor of all China. And Ting Ling and Princess Dar Ling were married immediately. And the first law that the new Emperor proclaimed was that the Empress Dar Ling should show her beauty to the people, so that all might know how fortunate China was in having such a lovely Empress.

And Ting Ling and Dar Ling ruled China wisely, and long and happy was their reign.

The Wonderful Knapsack

Retold by MARY C. HATCH

ONCE upon a time there was a soldier who had served his king well for ten years and a day, but alas, alack, when he came to get his pay for all the wars he had won, the king was as poor as he, and there were only three pennies left in the royal treasury.

"Well," said the soldier, "I'll not worry about it. I'll take my pay in honor and glory."

"To be sure," said the king, "honor and glory are all very well, but they'll not keep the wolf from the door. I will give you the palace plates. They are pure gold and will sell for a high price."

"Then you could not eat like a king," cried the soldier, "and that would never do. No indeed, your majesty, give me the three pennies and I will be on my way."

"Very well then," said the king, and he scooped up the three lone pennies from the bottom of the royal treasury and laid them in the hand of the soldier. "May they bring you luck," he said, and the soldier thanked him and went whistling on his way.

Now, when he had walked a mile or so, whom should he meet but an old, old crone, bent in the middle and with scarcely a tooth in her head.

"A penny from the young for the old," begged the old woman.

"A penny!" exclaimed the soldier. "Why, I've but three pennies in the whole, wide world. Still, it little matters if there are three or two," and so he gave the old woman one of the pennies.

Then he walked on another mile or so, till what should he come upon but a second old crone more bent and toothless than the first.

"A penny from the young for the old," begged the old woman.

"A penny!" cried the soldier. "Why, all I have in the whole, wide world is two pennies. Still, it little matters if there's two or one," and he gave the old woman the second of the pennies.

Then he walked on with the one lone penny, till after a mile or so he was stopped by a third old crone so bent that her chin almost touched her knees.

"A penny from the young for the old," said this old creature, and the soldier exclaimed, "One penny is all I have in the world. But it little matters if I've one or none," and he gave the last penny to the old woman.

At this, the old creature changed into a young and beautiful girl, for she was not really an old crone at all, but a fairy who had tested the soldier three times to see if he were good and brave.

"What a kind and generous lad you are," exclaimed the fairy. "And for that you deserve to be generously rewarded. I will give you three wishes, and all of them will come true."

But what do you know, the soldier could not think of a thing to wish for He had two strong arms, two long legs, and a head set straight on his shoulders, and that was all he had ever wanted. At length, however, he said, "I wish to have a long life and a healthy one."

"You have wished a good wish," said the fairy. "Now for your other wishes."

Now the soldier had a knapsack that had been with

him in the wars, and he liked the fit and the feel of it, particularly when it was full, so at last he said, "I wish that my knapsack will never wear out. And I wish last, that whatever I want will go into my knapsack, and whatever I want will come out."

"Three better wishes were never made," said the fairy, "nor three more easily granted. Now good-by, and good luck." And with that the fairy disappeared, and the soldier went happily on his way.

Toward evening he reached the town, and as he was very hungry, in he walked to the best inn and sat down at the finest table. "Landlord," he called, "serve me food, and serve it well," and the landlord came running.

But when the landlord saw a torn and tattered soldier instead of a silk and satin lord, he cried, "We will feed you food aplenty, good soldier, but you must come into the kitchen."

"No, thank you," said the soldier. "This will do quite nicely, I am sure. Of course, I am used to finer linen and brighter candlelight, but as I am hungry, it will not matter. Now bring me two bottles of your best wine and a dozen chicken breasts and be quick about it."

At this bold talk, the landlord quickly changed his tune,

for of course, no plain, ordinary soldier would speak in such a fashion, and this one must surely be a prince in disguise.

"Yes, sir, whatever you wish, sir," he said politely, and then he ran to set the table with his finest linen and dishes.

When all was ready, the soldier fell to eating at once, for he was quite famished, but near the end, he remembered to leave a good bit on his plate, since that, of course, is always what lords and ladies do. Then he wished a handful of gold coins into the knapsack, and taking out two of them, tossed them to the landlord.

"I trust this will pay for the meal," he said.

"It is payment, and more," said the landlord, and he bowed so low he bumped his head on the floor, "I hope everything suited your taste, your excellency."

"Fairly well, my good man," said the soldier. "Now you must provide me with a room for the night."

But alas, there were no rooms—and the landlord almost wept to say this—there were no rooms save one, and that could not be used.

"And why not?" exclaimed the soldier.

"Who goes in there alive comes out dead," cried the landlord.

"Is that all?" laughed the soldier. "Then that is the very room for me. Sweep it clean and make the bed well, for I am tired tonight."

The landlord wrung his hands, and the maids cried, and all the rich diners shook their heads, but nothing would do but that the soldier sleep in the dreadful room; and so it was prepared, and when the soldier had smoked awhile by the fire and felt a little drowsy, he bid everyone good night and went up to it.

Inside, he locked the door, stood his faithful knapsack in a corner where he could keep his eye on it, and sat down in a chair to see what would happen.

He had only a moment to wait until there was a great rustling in the chimney and a black ball came rolling out of the fireplace and into the center of the room. There it unrolled itself, and the soldier saw the ugliest troll ever seen in the whole, wide world, with eyes red as fire and fingers like claws. Then out rolled a second troll, and after that a third, each uglier than the next.

"How do you do?" said the soldier. "How very nice of you to come and keep me company! Now do sit down and make yourselves at home," and he pointed to three chairs on the other side of the fireplace

The three trolls seated themselves, but not for long. In
a minute they were up and at the soldier. One tweaked his
nose, the other pulled his ears, and the third one tried to
pin down his arms.

"Dear me," said the soldier, "I must say this is a strange way for guests to act. Well, if you can do no better, into my knapsack you must go." And there and then, into the knapsack they had to creep, and soon only a creaking and hissing could be heard.

"I hope you are comfortable there," said the soldier. "But if you are not, 'tis your own fault, to be sure. And now you must answer me a question. Why do you pester this room every night?"

There was a great silence for a moment, but whether they would or nay, the trolls had to give up their secret.

"We guard the oven," said the first.

"To protect a treasure," said the second.

"And woe to him who tries to steal it," said the third.

"Very well," said the soldier. "And thank you for your information." Then he undressed, for he was very tired, and went straight to bed.

Next morning the landlord, and the maids, and all the rich diners came to see what had happened to the remarkable soldier. They knocked on the door and peeked through the keyhole, but as the soldier was still sleeping he did not hear them, and so they thought he was dead and set up a great weeping and wailing.

"He was so young and handsome," cried all the maids.

"He was so rich," cried the landlord.

"And he ate like a prince," cried all the rich diners.

Now all this fuss and bother finally awakened the soldier, and he cried out crossly, "Landlord, landlord, what's all this fuss?"

"Oh, my!" cried everyone. "You're not still alive, are you?"

"Alive and ready to eat," answered the soldier. "Landlord, serve me a dozen fresh eggs and a pail of warm milk."

This the landlord ran to do, followed by the maids and diners, and when all was ready, the soldier got up and dressed, took a good look at his knapsack, then locked his room and went down to eat.

And when he had eaten, he commanded the landlord to bring him three strong men. "They must take my knapsack to the blacksmith's and beat the dust out of it," said the soldier. "I have walked a long mile or two in my day, and the knapsack is powerfully dusty."

The landlord did as he was ordered, though truth to tell, he considered it quite a strange request, and soon three strong men were lugging and tugging at the knapsack which looked light as a feather but weighed heavy as lead. And when they reached the blacksmith's shop, they were so tired they could hardly lift a finger, to say nothing of wielding a heavy hammer, so three of the blacksmith's strongest helpers were set to the task of beating the knapsack.

But what a shrieking was heard when they started their work, shrieking enough to set your hair on end!

"Don't mind a little noise," said the soldier. "My knapsack is a little squeaky at the seams. Just beat as hard as you can."

So the men went on, and after a while, all was quiet. Then the soldier said, "There, that's clean enough. Now be so good as to empty it into the sea."

But these poor fellows were now so tired they could scarce lift a finger, to say nothing of carrying a heavy knapsack down to the sea, so three more huskies were found, and they lugged and tugged till the strange knapsack was down to the shore. Then they opened it, and what a pile of black dust poured into the water! It was all good riddance, too, though it blackened the sea for a mile around.

The workmen were now paid for their hard labor, and

generously, too, with a handful of gold for each of them, and then the soldier returned to the landlord.

"Landlord," he cried, "I have one last task for you. In the room where I slept last night, there stands a big oven, and this you must tear down at once."

"Well," said the landlord to himself, "he'll soon want to pull down the roof from over my head, but I'll not question money." So he did as the soldier commanded, and there under the oven, what should he find but a pot of gold as big as a washtub!

"What a clever fellow you were to discover all this gold," exclaimed the landlord.

"Oh, 'twas nothing at all," said the soldier. "Now take it, good landlord, all of it, and use it well." Then he took up his knapsack and bid his host good-by. But the landlord would not let him go without half the money, and this he could not refuse. But it was a heavy load to carry, and so he must stay a bit longer. And then whom should he meet but the landlord's daughter, a very pretty lass, and so he must tarry still longer, till the lass was his bride, and then—well, with health, wealth, and happiness, he no doubt tarries there still.

Ashputtel

by WALTER DE LA MARE

THE wife of a rich man fell sick: and when she felt that her end drew nigh, she called her only daughter to her bedside, and said, "Always be a good girl; I love you dearly and I will look down from heaven and watch over you." Soon afterward she shut her eyes and died, and was buried not in the churchyard but in a wilderness of wild flowers at the far end of the garden. The little girl went every day to her grave and wept, and was always good and kind to all about her. Winter came; the snow spread its shining white coverlet over the grave; but by the time the sun had melted the snow away, her father had taken another wife.

This new wife had two daughters of her own, whom she brought with her: they were fair in face, but foul at heart, and it was now a sad and sorry time for the motherless little girl. "What is this good-for-nothing doing in the parlor?" they said. "They who would eat bread should first earn it; away with her to the kitchen!" They took away the pretty clothes her mother had made for her, gave her an ugly old frock to wear, laughed at her, and turned her into the kitchen.

There she was forced to do all the hard work; to rise before it was day, to fetch in water from the well, to lay the fire, to cook and to wash the clothes. Besides that, the two sisters plagued her in every way they could think of, teased, beat, and mocked at her. At night, when she was tired out, they gave her no bed to lie on, and she must needs sleep in the hearth among the ashes; and, as she was always dusty and dirty, they called her Ashputtel.

It happened one day that her father was going to the fair. Before he set out he asked his wife's daughters what he should bring them.

"Fine clothes," said the first.

"Pearls and diamonds," said the second.

"And you, child," said he to his own daughter, "what will you have?"

"The first sprig of any tree, dear father, that rubs against your hat on your way home," said she.

At the fair he bought for the two first the fine clothes and pearls and diamonds they had asked for: and on his way home, as he came riding through a green copse, a sprig of hazel brushed against his shoulder and almost pushed off his hat. It reminded him of his promise.

He broke off this hazel-sprig and brought it away with him; and when he came home he gave it to his daughter. She took it, went down to her mother's grave, and planted it there; and cried so much that it was watered with her tears. There it grew and flourished and became at length a tall leafy tree. Three times every day she visited it and wept; and one morning, in the spring, there came a small bird and built its nest in the tree, and talked with her, and watched over her, and brought her whatever she wished for.

Now some time afterwards it happened that the king of this country held a feast which was to last three days, and, out of those who were invited to come, his son was to choose a bride for himself. And Ashputtel's two sisters were bidden to the feast. On the first day they called her up from the kitchen and said, "Now, comb and dress our hair, polish our shoes, and tie our sashes for us, for we are going to dance at the king's feast." Ashputtel did as she was told, but when all was done and she was alone she could not help grieving; she was filled with such a longing to go to the dance too. At last she entreated her stepmother to let her go.

"You! Ashputtel?" she jeered. "You, who have nothing fit to wear, and cannot even dance—*you* want to go to the king's ball?"

And when Ashputtel kept on begging, her stepmother, merely to get rid of her, said at last, "Look, then; I will throw this basinful of peas on the ash heap; if you have picked every one of them out of it in an hour's time, you shall go to the feast." So she threw the basin of peas on-to the ashes and left her. Then Ashputtel ran out into the garden, and cried out:

> *"Hither, hither, through the sky,*
> *Turtle-dove and linnet, fly!*
> *Blackbird, thrush, and chaffinch gay,*
> *Hither, hither, haste away!*
> *All sweet birds, come help me quick,*
> *Hasten, hasten*—pick, pick, pick!"

And in a little while, first there came two wood-pigeons flying in at the kitchen window; next there came

two turtle-doves; and after these all the little birds under heaven came chirping and fluttering in, and flew down among the ashes. First the wood-pigeons stooped their heads and set to work, *pick, pick, pick;* and then the turtle-doves, and then all the other birds of every kind began to *pick, pick, pick.* Presently they had picked out every single pea, and had dropped them into the basin; there was not one pea left in the ashes.

Their work done, all the birds flew out at the kitchen window. Then Ashputtel brought the basin up to her stepmother, overjoyed at the thought that now she could go to the feast.

"What, you slattern!" cried her stepmother. "You, who have nothing but filthy rags to wear, and cannot even dance; *you* go to the ball! Away with you to your work!" And she drove her down to the kitchen.

Nevertheless, Ashputtel went on begging so hard to go, that, in order to be rid of her, her stepmother seized the basin and flung two whole basinfuls of peas on the ashes. "See here, then," she cried, "gather those up again, every one, in half an hour, and you shall go to the ball."

As soon as she was gone, Ashputtel ran out into the long garden, now full of the evening sun, and cried out as before:

> *"Hither, hither, through the sky,*
> *Turtle-dove and linnet, fly!*
> *Blackbird, thrush, and chaffinch gay*
> *Hither, hither, haste away!*
> *All sweet birds, come help me quick,*
> *Hasten, hasten—pick, pick, pick!"*

In less than half as many minutes as before, their work was done, and all the birds flew out at the kitchen window. And Ashputtel took up the two basins full to the

brim with peas to her stepmother, rejoicing at the thought
that now she should be able to go to the ball. But her
stepmother only flew into a passion. "What!" she shouted,
"shall I never be rid of you! Off to your cinders again,
and dance with the rats!" With that, she flung the basin
of peas in her face and drove her out of the room; and
she herself went off to the ball.

Now all were gone, and the house was empty. Weeping
bitterly, Ashputtel crept out into the garden and sat herself down under the nut tree over her mother's grave. She
fancied she heard a little stirring in its leaves. And,
"Oh," she cried in her heart,

> *"Green and shadowy hazel tree,*
> *Shed gold and silver over me!"*

Instantly, with a song of joy, the bird flew up out of
the tree, to return in a while, first with a dress of gold
and silver, and presently after with slippers of spangled
silk. Ashputtel lost not a moment. She washed herself in
the cold well water, put on the dress of gold and silver
and the slippers of spangled silk, and followed her sisters
to the feast at the king's palace.

When she came into the ballroom, her stepmother and

sisters did not recognize her. They thought this must be some strange princess from a far country, she looked so lovely. Never once did they give a thought to Ashputtel, supposing only she was long ago fast asleep in her kitchen among the ashes.

At first sight of her, the king's son came up to her, took her by the hand, and danced with her. He never left her side, and danced with no one else the whole long evening through.

When midnight struck, Ashputtel told the prince that she must go home.

"Come, then," he said, "we will go together, and I will take care of you." For his one desire was to see where she lived. But she slipped away from him unawares, and ran off as fast as she could, the prince following after her. When she came back at last to the garden, she ran up the steps in the moonlight into the pigeon house, and shut the door behind her, answering never a word. There the prince stayed until her father came home. He then told him what had happened—how he had pursued an unknown and beautiful maiden who had danced with him at the feast; and that she had hidden herself in the pigeon house.

They broke open the door of the pigeon house, but found only the doves there, awakened from sleep. Else, it was empty. On their return, they passed through the kitchen; and there, among the ashes and in her old ragged clothes, her dim little lamp still burning in the chimney, lay Ashputtel, seemingly fast asleep. As quickly as she could, she had climbed out through a hole in the roof of the pigeon house, and on to the hazel tree, whose branches reached its upper wall. Having stripped off her dress of gold and silver, and taken off her slippers of spangled silk, she had put them under the hazel tree so that the bird might carry them away. Then she had put on her old gray frock, and had lain down among the ashes.

On the second day of the feast, when her father and mother and sisters had gone, and the long day's work was over, Ashputtel went again to the hazel tree, and cried:

"Shake, shake, hazel tree,
Gold and silver over me!"

The bird came at once to her call, bringing with it a dress even rarer and finer than the one she had worn the night before. When Ashputtel came into the ballroom, everyone there marveled at her beauty, and the king's son, who had been awaiting her, took her by the hand and danced with her, refusing to give her up, no matter who might plead to dance with her.

When midnight came, she entreated him to let her go home, and she sped away. But he followed her swiftly, burning to see from whence she had come. As fast as she could run, she came in the moonlight to the wall of the garden of her father's house, scrambled over it, and having nowhere else to hide, climbed up breathlessly into the branches of a great pear tree, already dangling with its ripening fruit. There she hid herself among the leaves.

The king's son sought in vain for her; watched until her father came home from the feast; and then said to him, "The lovely stranger who danced with me all the evening has slipped away again, and I think she must have hidden herself in yonder pear tree."

For an instant her father thought within himself, "Can this stranger be my daughter Ashputtel?" But he put it out of his mind and said nothing. He gave orders that an ax should be brought and the pear tree cut down; but, apart from its fruit, there was nothing to be seen in its branches. When they returned to the kitchen, there lay Ashputtel in the ashes as usual; for the moment the prince had turned away, she had slipped down on the other side of the pear tree, and having hidden her clothes at the foot of the hazel tree, had hastened back to her kitchen.

The next evening she again whispered to her hazel tree:

"Shake, shake, hazel tree,
Gold and silver over me!"

and the bird brought her a dress even richer and rarer and finer than the last; and slippers of gold.

When for the third time she came into the great room in the king's palace, no one could find words to express their wonder at her beauty. The king's son danced with her the whole evening, and would allow no one else a minute of her company. When midnight struck once more, he vowed to himself, "Not this time, not *this* time shall she escape me."

None the less, Ashputtel contrived to slip away from him, though in her haste she left behind her one of her golden slippers on the stairs. The prince himself found the slipper; went the next day to the king, his father, and said, "I will take to wife the lady whose left foot fits this golden slipper, and her alone." So the king made a proclamation.

Ashputtel's stepsisters rejoiced to hear it. They flattered themselves they had slim and beautiful feet, and had no doubt they could wear the golden slipper. The elder went first into the room to try on the slipper; and her mother stood by watching. But try as she would, her great toe refused to go into it. By the length and breadth of her great toe the slipper was too small for her. Then the mother gave her a knife, and said, "What, one toe in the way! Cut it off, daughter. When you are queen, you will never need to fret yourself about one toe more or less, since you will never go out on foot."

So the silly girl cut off her great toe, squeezed on the

slipper, and limped downstairs and out to where the king's son was waiting. He gazed at her in dismay, but the golden slipper fitted. He kept his word, set her up behind him on his horse, and rode away.

In a little while he came riding along beside the garden wall and not far from where, on the other side of it, grew the hazel tree that Ashputtel had planted. And in the silence of the morning there sat a bird on the branches of the tree, and this is what it sang:

"Turn again! Turn again! Look to your shoe!
It's a toe's length too small, and was not made for you!
Turn again, Prince! Look elsewhere for thy bride,
A cheat and deceiver sits there at thy side."

On hearing this, the prince immediately dismounted, and examined the slipper that hung beside his stirrup. It was dripping wet with blood. And he saw the trick that had been played on him. He turned his horse about, brought the false creature back to her father's house, and said, "This is not the lady I am seeking. Let her sister try on the slipper."

So the younger sister went into the room with her mother to put it on. The five toes slipped in easily, every

one; but not her heel. By her heel's length and breadth
the slipper was too small for her. Her mother, watching
her, fell into a rage. By hook and by crook, she pushed
and squeezed her daughter's heel into the slipper until
the blood came; then she took the girl down to the king's
son. He set her behind him on his horse, and once again
rode away.

In a little while, they came again to the hazel tree. The
bird was still perched among its branches; and again it
sang out:

"Turn again! Turn again! Look to your shoe!
It's a heel's length too small, and was not made for you!
Turn again, Prince! Look elsewhere for thy bride,
A cheat and deceiver sits there at thy side."

Again he dismounted, and so much blood had come
oozing from the heel of the sister that now sat behind his
saddle that her white stocking was dyed red with it. So
he turned his horse about again and brought her back.
"Neither is this the lady I am seeking," he said to her
father; "have you no other daughter?"

"None," said he, "except only a poor drudge who works
in the kitchen and whom we call Ashputtel. She is the

child of my first wife, and lay asleep in the kitchen when I returned after the feast."

None the less, the prince bade him send for her. At this her stepmother cried out, "No, no, she is a slattern; and much too dirty to show herself. She will not dare to appear."

But the prince insisted on seeing her, and she was brought up from the kitchen.

Just as she was, she came into the room and curtsied to the prince. He knelt before her, took off the clumsy wooden shoe from her left foot, and put on the golden slipper. Heel to toe, it fitted perfectly.

He looked closely into her face, and his heart went out to her.

"This is the lady," he said, "whom these many days I have been seeking—and seeking in vain."

On hearing this, the stepmother and her daughters turned ashen pale with fear and rage, but dared utter never a word. They watched from the window as the prince lifted Ashputtel on to his horse and rode away with her.

When the two of them came to the hazel tree, the bird perched among its leaves sang out:

"Home, now! Home, again! Look at the shoe!
Princess! 'twas I who brought it to you.
Prince! hie away with thy beautiful bride,
She alone is thy loved one and sits at thy side!"

Its song finished, it fluttered down from the hazel tree and alighted on Ashputtel's shoulder. And so they went on together.

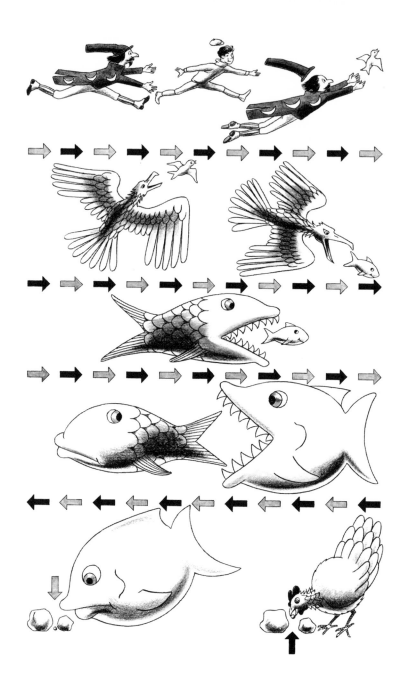

The Sorcerer's Apprentice

Freely translated by WANDA GÁG
from Grimm's Tales

A MAN found himself in need of a helper for his workshop, and one day as he was walking along the outskirts of a little hamlet he met a boy with a bundle slung over his shoulder. Stopping him, the man said, "Good morning, my lad. I am looking for an apprentice. Have you a master?"

"No," said the boy, "I have just this morning said good-by to my mother and am now off to find myself a trade."

"Good," said the man. "You look as though you might be just the lad I need. But wait, do you know anything about reading and writing?"

"Oh yes!" said the boy.

"Too bad!" said the man. "You won't do after all. I have no use for anyone who can read and write."

"Pardon me?" said the boy. "If it was *reading* and *writing* you were talking about, I misunderstood you. I thought you asked if I knew anything about *eating* and *fighting*—those two things I am able to do well, but as to reading and writing, that is something I know nothing about."

"Well!" cried the man. "Then you are just the fellow I want. Come with me to my workshop, and I will show you what to do."

The boy, however, had his wits about him. He could read and write well enough and had only pretended to be a fool. Wondering why a man should prefer to have an unschooled helper, he thought to himself, "I smell a rat. There is something strange about this, and I had better keep my eyes and ears open."

While he was pondering over this, his new master was leading him into the heart of a deep forest. Here in a small clearing stood a house and, as soon as they entered it, the boy could see that this was no ordinary workshop.

At one end of a big room was a huge hearth with a copper cauldron hanging in it; at the other end was a small alcove lined with many big books. A mortar and pestle stood on a bench; bottles and sieves, measuring scales and oddly shaped glassware were strewn about on the table.

Well! It did not take the clever young apprentice very long to realize that he was working for a magician or sorcerer of some kind, and so, although he pretended to be quite stupid, he kept his eyes and ears open, and tried to learn all he could.

"Sorcery—that is a trade I would dearly love to master!" said the boy to himself. "A mouthful of good chants and charms would never come amiss to a poor fellow like me, and with them I might even be able to do some good in the world."

There were many things the boy had to do. Sometimes he was ordered to stir the evil-smelling broths which bubbled in the big copper cauldron; at other times he had to grind up herbs and berries—and other things too gruesome to mention—with the big mortar and pestle. It was also his task to sweep up the workshop, to keep the fire burning in the big hearth, and to gather the strange materials needed by the man for the broths and brews he was always mixing.

This went on day after day, week after week, and month after month, until the boy was almost beside himself with curiosity. He was most curious about the thick heavy books in the alcove. How often he had wondered about them, and how many times had he been tempted to take a peep between their covers! But, remembering that he was not supposed to know how to read or write, he had been wise enough never to show the least interest in them. At last there came a day when he made up his mind to see what was in them, no matter what the risk.

"I'll try it before another day dawns," he thought.

That night he waited until the sorcerer was sound asleep and was snoring loudly in his bedchamber; then, creeping out of his straw couch, the boy took a light into the corner of the alcove and began paging through one of the heavy volumes. What was written in them has never been told, but they were conjuring books, each and every one of them; and from that time on, the boy read in them silently, secretly, for an hour or two, night after night. In this way he learned many magic tricks: chants, and charms and countercharms; recipes for philters and potions, for broths and brews and witches' stews; signs mystic and cabalistic, and other helpful spells of many kinds. All these he memorized carefully, and it was not long before he sometimes was able to figure out what kind of charms his master was working, what brand of potion he was mixing, what sort of stews he was brewing. And what kind of charms and potions and stews were they? Alas, they were all wicked ones! Now the boy knew that he was working not for an ordinary magician, but a cruel, dangerous sorcerer. And because of this, the boy made a plan, a bold one.

He went on with his nightly studies until his head was swarming with magic recipes and incantations. He even had time to work at them in the daytime, for the sorcerer sometimes left the workshop for hours—working harm and havoc on mortals, no doubt. At such times the boy would try out a few bits of his newly learned wisdom. He began with simple things, such as changing the cat into a bee and back to a cat again, making a viper out of the poker, an imp out of the broom, and so on. Sometimes he was successful, often he was not; so he said to himself, "The time is not yet ripe."

One day, after the sorcerer had again gone forth on one of his mysterious trips, the boy hurried through his work, and had just settled himself in the dingy alcove with one of the conjuring books on his knees, when the master returned unexpectedly. The boy, thinking fast, pointed smiling at one of the pictures, after which he quietly closed the book and went on with his work as though nothing were amiss.

But the sorcerer was not deceived.

"If the wretch can read," he thought, "he may learn how to outwit me. And I can't send him off with a beating and a 'bad speed to you,' either—doubtless he knows too much already and will reveal all my fine mean tricks, and then I can't have any more sport working mischief on man and beast."

He acted quickly.

With one leap he rushed at the boy, who in turn made a spring for the door.

"Stop!" cried the sorcerer. "You shall not escape me!" He was about to grab the boy by the collar when the quick-witted lad mumbled a powerful incantation by which he changed himself into a bird, and—Whoosh!—he had flown into the woods.

The sorcerer, not to be outdone, shouted a charm, thus changing himself into a larger bird—and Whoosh!—he was after the little one.

With a new incantation the boy made himself into a fish—and Whish!—he was swimming across a big pond.

But the master was equal to this, for with a few words he made himself into a fish too, a big one, and swam after the little one.

At this the boy changed himself into a still bigger fish, but the magician, by a master stroke, turned himself into a tiny kernel of grain and rolled into a small crack in a stone where the fish couldn't touch him.

Quickly the boy changed himself into a rooster, and— *Peck! Peck! Peck!*—with his sharp beak he snapped at the kernel of grain and ate it up.

That was the end of the wicked sorcerer, and the boy became the owner of the magic workshop. And wasn't it fine that all the powers and ingredients which had been used for evil by the sorcerer were now in the hands of a boy who would use them only for the good of man and beast?

The Dutiful Daughter

by KATHARINE PYLE

THERE once lived in Korea a rich merchant and his wife who had no children, though they greatly desired them and prayed every day that a child might be granted them.

They had been married sixteen years and were no longer young, when the wife had a wonderful dream. In her dream she walked in a garden full of beauteous fruits and flowers and singing birds, and as she walked, suddenly a star fell from heaven into her bosom.

As soon as the wife awoke, she told this dream to her husband. "I feel assured," said she, "that this dream can mean only one thing, and that is that heaven is about to send us a child, and that this child will be as a star for beauty and wonder and grace."

The merchant could hardly believe that this good fortune was really to be theirs; but it was indeed as the wife had said, and in due time a daughter was born to the couple, and this child was so beautiful that she was the wonder of all who saw her.

The husband and wife, who had hoped for a son, were greatly disappointed that the long-wished-for child was only a daughter, but their disappointment was soon forgotten in the joy and pride they felt in her beauty and wit and goodness.

Unhappily, while Sim Ching (for so the girl was named) was still a child, her mother died, and her father's grief over the loss of his wife was so great that he became completely blind. He was now obliged to leave the most of his business affairs in the hands of his servants, and these servants were so dishonest and so idle that they either wasted or stole all his money. At last he became so poor that he could scarcely provide enough food to keep himself and his daughter alive.

One day the merchant in his unhappiness wandered away from home, and being blind and so unable to tell where he was going, he fell into a deep pit out of which he was unable to climb.

He feared he would die there, but presently, hearing

footsteps on the road above, he called out for help.

The footsteps he heard were those of a greedy and dishonest official who lived near by. Every day he passed this way on his walks. Hearing the voice from the pit, the official went to the edge of it. Looking down into it, he saw the blind man there below.

"Who are you?" asked the official, "and how have you fallen into this pit?"

"I am a poor blind man, who was once a rich merchant," replied the man in the pit. "I lost at once both my sight and my wealth, and because I cannot see I fell into this pit from which I am not able to climb. For the sake of mercy reach down your hand and draw me out."

"Not so," replied the official. "That would be a foolish thing for me to do. Instead of drawing you out, I might myself be pulled in. But if you will promise to give me a hundred and fifty bags of rice that I may offer them up in the temple, I will go and get a rope and throw the end of it down to you, and by that means I may be able to pull you out without danger to either of us."

The official asked for the rice for the temple not because he really wished to make an offering of it, for indeed he meant to keep it for himself, but he thought, "If this man was once rich, no doubt he must still know some wealthy people, and if he goes to them and asks for rice to offer up in the temple they will be more likely to give it to him than if he told them it was for me."

When the poor man heard that the official demanded his promise of a hundred and fifty bags of rice before he would help him, he cried aloud with grief and wonder.

"How is it possible I should promise you such a thing as that?" he cried. "None but a very rich man could make such a gift to the temple, and I am so poor that I cannot even provide food enough for myself and my daughter."

"Your daughter!" cried the official. "You have then a daughter?"

"Yes; and she is so beautiful that no one in the whole land can compare with her for fairness, and she is as good as she is beautiful, and as witty as she is good."

"Now listen!" said the official. "If you will swear to give me the bags of rice, not only will I pull you out of the pit, but I foresee that because of this gift your daughter will be raised to the highest place in the land, and you yourself will receive great wealth and honor, and your sight will return to you."

This the official said, not because he really foresaw anything of the kind, but because he wished to tempt the blind man into making him the promise of the rice.

The poor man still declared that he had no means of making such an offering, but the official urged and begged and threatened, until at last the blind merchant gave his promise.

The official then ran and got a rope, and soon pulled the blind merchant out of the pit.

"Now remember!" said he. "Exactly a month from now I will send my servants for the rice, and you must in some way have it ready, whether you beg or borrow or steal it, and if you do not, you shall receive a good beating for breaking your bargain with me, and be thrown into a prison that is worse than any pit."

The blind man returned home, very sad and sorrowful.

As soon as he entered the door, his daughter saw by his look that something unfortunate had happened and begged him to tell her what it was.

At first he would not say because he feared to frighten her, but she asked him so many questions that at last he was obliged to tell her the whole story.

Sim Ching was indeed terrified when she heard what her father had promised.

"Alas! Alas!" she cried. "How can we possibly get the rice ready for him? You know it is only by the kindness of the neighbors that we have the handful that I have cooked for our dinner today."

The poor man began to weep. "What you say is true," he cried. "Better that I should have died in the pit than be thrown into prison, as will surely happen to me if I cannot give him the hundred and fifty bags that I promised him."

The blind man now set out to beg, telling everyone his sad story and asking them to help him to collect the rice, but the people of the village were themselves poor and had no more than enough food for their own families.

Time slipped by, until at last the day arrived when the official's servants were to come to demand the rice. The blind man had not yet been able to get together even one bagful of rice, let alone a hundred and fifty.

He and his daughter sat together very sorrowful, and now and then the blind man bemoaned himself as he thought of how he was to be beaten and thrown into prison, for he had now learned enough about the official to know that he could expect no mercy from one as cruel and greedy as he.

The Dutiful Daughter

Now there lived in another city, not far away, a very rich merchant who owned many ships that traded in foreign lands. This merchant had become so proud of his wealth and his power that he called himself the Prince of the Sea, and so it was that he obliged others to address him. This greatly offended a powerful Water Spirit who lived under the sea over which the ships of the merchant sailed. And now, in order to punish the merchant, the Water Spirit sent storms down upon the ships. Many were destroyed, and others were driven onto reefs, or back to the ports they sailed from. So many misfortunes overtook the vessels that sailors became afraid to sail on them, and the merchant feared he would be ruined.

In his trouble he sent for a number of wise men and magicians and asked them why he was now so unlucky, and what he could do to bring back good fortune.

The wise men and magicians studied their books and consulted together for a long time, and then they came to the merchant and said, "We have found why you are so unlucky. Your pride has offended a powerful Water Spirit, and it is he who is wrecking your ships or driving them back into port. There is only one way in which to turn aside his anger. If a young and beautiful maiden can

be found who will willingly offer herself as a sacrifice to him, then he will be satisfied and will punish you no further. Otherwise he will certainly destroy every vessel you send out, and so in the end you will be ruined."

When the merchant heard this, he was in despair. "Now indeed there is no hope for me," he cried, "for I am very sure there is not, in the whole of Korea, a maiden who would be willing to be sacrificed to this Water Spirit, however great the reward I might offer. For indeed, of what use would any reward be to her, if in order to gain it she must be drowned in the sea?"

However, his head steward, who had charge of his affairs, begged him at least to send out a proclamation and to offer a reward to the family of any maiden who would consent to the sacrifice. "It may be that such a one will be found," said he; "—someone who values the fortunes of her parents even above her own life."

The merchant finally agreed to the wishes of his steward, and messengers were sent forth to read the proclamation aloud in every city, town, and village in the country. They went this way and that, east, west, north, and south, and finally one of them came to the place where the blind man and his daughter lived. The day the mes-

senger came to the village was the very day when the servants of the wicked official were to come and demand the
hundred and fifty bags of rice from the blind man.

The merchant's messenger took his stand not far from
the blind man's house, and from there he read aloud the
proclamation as to the sacrifice and the reward that would
be paid to the parents of any maiden who would be willing to be thrown to the Water Spirit.

The man was already turning away when Sim Ching
asked a woman who was standing near what the man had
been saying. The woman told her, laughing as she spoke.
"How could anyone suppose that any maiden would consent to be thrown to this monster in order that her family
might have the reward!" cried the woman.

But Sim Ching ran after the man and caught him by
the sleeve.

"Wait," cried she. "Do not go until you have told me
something. You say your master will richly reward the
family of any maiden who will willingly give herself to
this Water Spirit. Would he give as much as a hundred
and fifty bags of rice to such a family?"

"That and more," replied the messenger. "My master is
very rich, and the reward will be generous."

"Then I will go with you and be the sacrifice," said Sim Ching. "Permit me only to go and bid farewell to my father, and then I will be ready."

The messenger rejoiced that he had been able to secure the maiden for his master and gladly consented to wait until she had spoken with her father.

But when Sim Ching went back into the house and told her father what she intended to do he was in despair. He wept aloud and rent his clothes. "Never, never will I consent to such a sacrifice," cried he.

But his daughter comforted him. "Do you forget," said she, "what the official promised you? Did he not tell you that if you offered up this rice to the temple, all would be well with us, and that I would be raised to the highest place in the kingdom? Let us have faith and believe that the gods of the temple can save me at the last even though I be thrown into the sea."

As her father listened to her, he grew quieter, and at last gave his consent for her to go. The neighbors who had heard what she meant to do gathered about to bid her farewell and could not but weep for pity, even while they praised her for her dutifulness toward her father.

Sim Ching at once set out with the messenger, who was

in haste to bring her before his master. Indeed he feared that if she thought too long of what she had consented to do, she might repent of her bargain.

When he reached the merchant's house and told him he had found a maiden for the sacrifice, his master could scarcely believe him. "Does she understand what is required of her, and is she willing?" he asked. The messenger assured him that she understood perfectly and rejoiced at the thought of securing the reward for her father.

Sim Ching was now brought before the merchant, and when he saw her beauty and youth and her modest, gentle air, he was filled with pity for her. He would even have commanded that she should be taken back again to her father, but to this Sim Ching would not consent.

"No," said she. "I have come here to do a certain thing. I have promised, and I do not wish to break my word. All I ask is to be assured that the bags of rice will certainly be sent to my father, and that at once."

"Let it then be as you desire," said the merchant. "And be assured that my part of the bargain shall be kept as faithfully as yours." He then ordered that one hundred and fifty bags of rice should be loaded on as many mules and sent to the blind man at once, that Sim Ching might herself have the comfort of seeing them set forth.

This was done, and after the train of mules had departed, Sim Ching was taken to a chamber where magnificent robes and veils and jewels had been laid ready for her. Her attendants dressed her and hung the jewels on her neck and arms, and when all was done, she was so beautiful that even the attendants wept to think she must be sacrificed.

A barge had been made ready and hung about with garlands, and in it sat musicians to make sweet music while the rowers rowed to where the sacrifice was to be made.

And now Sim Ching would have been afraid, but she fixed her thoughts upon her father and on how he would now be saved from the cruelty of the official, and then she became quite happy and was no longer frightened.

When the barge came to the place under which the Water Spirit lived, Sim Ching leaned over the side of the boat and looked down into the water. It was very deep and green, and it seemed to her that beneath she could see shining walls and towers, as though of some great castle, and that the spirits of the water were beckoning to her to come. Lower and lower she leaned, until, as though drawn by some power beneath, she sank over the side of the vessel and down and down through the water until she was lost to the sight of those above her.

Then the rowers took the barge back to the shore and told the merchant the sacrifice had been accepted. The merchant was glad that now again his ships might sail in safety; but at the same time he felt pity for Sim Ching, believing she had been drowned.

But such was not the case. After she had sunk down and down through the waters for what seemed to her a long distance, she came to the land where the Water Spirit is King. All about her were things strange and beautiful. There were water weeds so tall they were like trees waving high above her, and through them, like birds, darted the shining fishes. There were water flowers of colors she had never seen before, and shining shells, and before her rose a castle made of mother-of-pearl and studded with precious stones that shone and glittered like stars in the light that came down through the water.

While she was looking at it, the doors of the castle swung open, and a train of attendants came out to meet her. These attendants were all dressed in green, and many

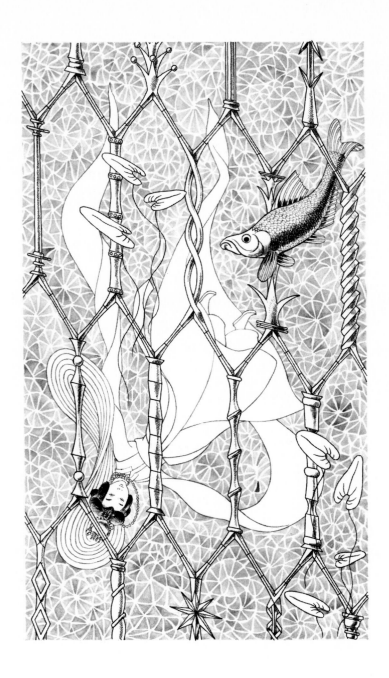

of them would have been very handsome except that they themselves were green. Their faces, their hands, their hair, and eyes—everything about them was green.

They spoke to Sim Ching in a strange language, but soon she understood them and knew they had come to bring her before their King who was waiting for her. Sim Ching felt no doubt but that this King was the Water Spirit himself, and she was very much frightened, but still she did not hesitate, but went with them willingly, for it was for this purpose she had come.

The attendants led her through one room after another, until they came to the place where the Water Spirit sat upon a crystal throne, and he, too, was green, but his crown was of gold, and his garments were set all over with pearls and precious stones.

The King looked at Sim Ching kindly and bade her have no fear. "I intend you no harm," said he, "and indeed I wished for no sacrifice. My only wish was to punish the rich merchant for his pride, and so it was that I set him a task that I thought impossible for him to perform. But because of your dutifulness and your love for your father, he has been able to make the sacrifice. Now you must stay here patiently for a year and teach the sea-

maidens the ways of the world above, and at the end of
that time you shall return to the earth, and receive the
happiness you deserve."

Sim Ching listened to him, wondering, and when he
had made an end of speaking, she gladly agreed to serve
for a time in the palace and to teach the sea-people all
she knew. So for a twelvemonth Sim Ching stayed there
and was very happy, for though the ways and manners of
the sea-people were strange to her, they themselves were
kind and gentle, so that she soon lost all fear of them.

At the end of the twelve months, the King sent for
Sim Ching, and when she had come before him, he said,
"Sim Ching, for a year you have served us faithfully and
well, and now the time has come for you to return to the
upper world. But in that world there are many dangers,
and you have no one to protect you. I have, therefore,
caused a great flower to be prepared for you. When you
enter into this flower, the leaves will fold about you and
hide you, so that none may suspect you are within it. The
leaves will afford you food and drink as well as shelter.
In this way you can live protected and in safety until fate
sends you a husband to love and guard you."

After speaking thus, the Water Spirit led Sim Ching

into another room and there showed her the flower that he had caused to be prepared for her. This flower was very large and of a beautiful rose color, and the leaves were of some rich, thick substance that had a most delicious smell and was good to eat. The juice of the leaves also afforded a delicious drink. Sim Ching, as she examined it, knew not how to express her wonder and admiration.

The King bade her step into the flower. She did so, and at once the leaves closed about her, so that she was completely hidden, and at the same time the most delightful music breathed softly from the flower. It now floated softly up and up, through the roof of the palace, and through the waters above, until it reached the surface of the sea. There it rested, rocking gently with the motion of the waves.

Now it so happened that the place where the flower floated on the sea was not far from the palace of the young King of that country. The morning it arose through the waters, the King was looking from a window across the sea toward a pleasure island where he sometimes went. Suddenly, between himself and the island, he saw something glittering in the sunlight out upon the waters.

He could not make out what the object was, and he

ordered that some of the castle servants should row out to it, see what it was, and if possible bring it back with them. This was done, and when the rowers returned they brought the flower with them and carried it in to where the young King was awaiting them.

When the King saw the flower, he was filled with wonder and admiration. Never before had he seen such a blossom. He examined it on all sides and exclaimed over its size and beauty.

"It must be some magic," said he, "that has created such a flower. A room shall be built for it, and there I will keep it, and if indeed it has been made by magic, as I suspect, it may be that in time some fruit will come from it that will be even more beautiful than the flower itself."

The room that was now prepared for the flower was so magnificent that no other apartment in the palace could compare with it. The walls were of gold, overlaid with paintings and hung with silken embroidered hangings. The floors were set with precious stones. There were fountains, and couches heaped with soft cushions, and from the ceiling hung seven alabaster lamps that were kept burning both night and day.

When the room was finished, the King caused the

flower to be carefully carried into it and placed in the center upon a raised dais covered with embroidered velvet. After this no one was allowed to enter the room except himself, and he carried the key of it hung on a jeweled chain about his neck. Every day he spent long hours with the flower admiring its beauty, enjoying its delicious perfume, and listening to the delicate music that sometimes breathed out from among its leaves.

All the while Sim Ching lay hidden in the center of the flower without the King's once suspecting it. All day the leaves were closed about her, and only at night did they open to allow her to come forth.

The first time they unfolded, she was very much surprised to find herself in a room of a palace, instead of out upon the sea as she had supposed. Wondering, she stepped from the flower and began, timidly, to examine the apartment to which she had been brought. The beauty of it delighted her. She rested among the soft cushions, and bathed in the fountains, and dressed her hair. But toward morning she re-entered the flower, and the leaves closed about her so that she was again hidden from view.

For some time life went on in this manner. All day Sim Ching slept in the flower, and only at night did she

come forth, and as the King only visited the room in the daytime he never saw her, nor even guessed that a living maiden was inclosed by the leaves of the flower he admired so greatly.

But it so happened that one night the King could not sleep, and he took a fancy to visit the flower and see it by the light of the lamps. He therefore made his way along the corridors, and fitting the key into the lock, he turned it without having made a sound.

What was his surprise, when he opened the door, to see a maiden of surpassing beauty sitting beside a fountain and amusing herself by catching the water in her hands. When Sim Ching saw the King she gave a cry, and would have run back into the flower to hide, but the King called to her gently, bidding her stay.

"I will not harm you," said he. "But tell me who you are and how you have come here. It must be you are some spirit or fairy, for no human being could be as beautiful as you."

"I am no spirit, nor am I a fairy," answered Sim Ching, "but only the daughter of a poor blind beggar, and as to how I came here I know not." Sim Ching then told him her history from the time her father had become blind and fallen into the pit, to the hour when the Water Spirit had bade her enter the flower and the leaves closed about her.

The young King listened and wondered. "Yours is indeed a strange story," said he, "and this mischievous official shall be sought out and punished as he deserves. And yet it may be his promises shall all come true, and you shall indeed be exalted one day to the highest place in the kingdom."

He then told Sim Ching he loved her and desired nothing in the world so much as to make her his wife. To this Sim Ching joyfully consented, for the young King was so handsome and gracious, and spoke so well and wisely, that she could not but love him with all her heart, even as he loved her.

All night they sat and talked together, and in the morning he opened the door of the chamber and led her forth, and called the courtiers and nobles together, and told them she was to be his bride. Then there was great rejoicing, and everyone who saw Sim Ching wondered at her beauty and loved her for her gentle and gracious manner.

Soon after, she and the King were married, and they loved each other so dearly that Sim Ching would have been perfectly happy except for the thought of her old father and his griefs and sorrows.

Immediately after she was married, she sent messengers to the village where she had lived, bidding them find her father and bring him to her, but the old man had disappeared, and no one knew what had become of him.

Then the Queen had a great feast prepared and sent word throughout the length and breadth of the kingdom that all who were both poor and blind were bidden to the palace to eat of it. All would be welcome, and none should be turned away.

Then from far and near the blind and poor came flocking to the palace, scores and hundreds of them. The tables for the feast were laid in a great hall, and the young King and Queen sat on raised thrones at one end of it. All who came to the feast were obliged to pass before this throne before they might take their places at the table, and as each one passed, the Queen looked at him eagerly, hoping to recognize her father, but none of all the multitude was the one she sought. At last every one was seated; the attendants were about to close the doors, when another beggar, the last of all, came stumbling into the hall. He was so feeble and so old that he could scarcely make his way to the throne, but no sooner did the Queen see him than she knew him as her father.

Then she gave a great cry, and came down from the throne, and threw her arms about him, and wept over him.

"It is I, oh, my father! It is thy daughter, Sim Ching," she wept.

Then her father knew her voice and cried aloud with joy. "Oh, my daughter, I had thought thee dead," he cried, "and now thou art alive and I can feel thy arms about me." As he spoke the tears of joy ran down his cheeks, and these tears washed away the mists of sorrow that had clouded his eyes and he found he could see again.

Then there was great rejoicing, and the King called the old man father and made him welcome, and in due time he who had been blind and now could see was raised to great wealth and honor, and so the words of the official, that he had spoken without believing, came true.

The Three Wishes

by BARBARA LEONIE PICARD

THE old basketmaker in the village had two appren-
tices. They had been with him since they were boys, and
as they were both orphans they lived with the basketmaker's family. They were two fine, honest, hard-working
young men called Gregory and John, and at the time this
story begins they were both just twenty years old. Gregory was ambitious and hoped one day to live in the town
and own a large basket shop and have at least ten appren-
tices, but John, who was a more simple fellow, declared
himself quite content to become a master basketmaker in
the village.

Every week, on market day, Gregory or John would
take the baskets they had made to the neighboring town
and sell them, returning in the evening with a purse full
of silver and copper pieces for his master.

Castles and Dragons

One fine evening in late summer, as Gregory was making his way home from the market, he decided to take the path through the wood instead of keeping to the road. "For," he thought, "even if it is not a short cut, it will be pleasant in the wood at this time of year, and the birds are singing very merrily among the trees."

When he was well into the wood he suddenly heard sounds of lamentation, and saw before him an old woman sitting on a large basket filled with fir cones and pieces of wood, wringing her hands. She was surely the ugliest old woman in the world and she was dressed in filthy rags.

"What ails you, mother?" asked the young man.

"Alas, alas, kind sir, I must be out of the wood by sundown, and I can carry my basket no farther, for I am tired."

"That is easily remedied," laughed Gregory. "Stand up and I will carry it for you." But when he came to lift the basket he found it as heavy as if it had been filled with lead.

"Mercy on us, mother," he exclaimed, "it feels as though it were full of lead, I cannot think how you carried it a single step," and with a great effort he heaved it onto his back and staggered off under his load, the old woman walking by his side.

"Hurry, hurry, lad, for I must be out of the wood by sundown, and it lacks but thirty minutes till then."

"Never fret, old lady, we will be out of the wood by then."

But she kept urging him to hurry and seemed so afraid to be in the wood at dusk that Gregory hurried as fast as he could with his burden. To make matters worse, every few seconds the old woman would dart forward and pick up another piece of wood or another fir cone and put it into the basket on Gregory's back, saying, "Here is another fine cone to keep a poor old woman warm," or, "I must have this piece as well, for I shall not be able to collect any more firewood before the winter is upon us," and each fir cone and each piece of wood that she added to the basket was like another pound of lead to carry.

"In a moment," thought Gregory, "my back will be broken, but I cannot tell the poor old soul to stop picking up any more wood; it would be unkind, as she surely needs it. The marvel is that the basket can hold any more, for it was full to the brim when I picked it up."

And so they went on, Gregory struggling along with

the basket on his back, and the old woman by his side, picking up fresh pieces of wood for him to carry, and continually urging him on. He did not like to stop for a rest because he knew that she would be distressed by the waste of time, and as it drew nearer to sunset she became more and more impatient, upbraiding him for his slowness and almost screaming at him in her impatience.

"You clumsy great oaf! Can you not hurry a little? Must you crawl along?"

So that it was all that Gregory could do not to lose his temper with her and tell her to hold her tongue or else carry her own basket.

At last, after what seemed more like half a day than half an hour, they reached the edge of the wood just as the sun disappeared behind the hills, and with a sigh of relief Gregory set down the basket.

"I told you that I would get you out in time, mother," he said, turning to her with a smile. But the old woman had gone, and in her place stood a tall and beautiful lady, dressed in a shining robe, with a glowing crown upon her head. She smiled at Gregory. "I am the Queen of the Woods," she said, "and sometimes it pleases me to seek for a mortal who is kind and patient that he may have the reward which he deserves. In return for your kindness to an old woman, I give you three wishes. Use them well." And before Gregory could even thank her, she had vanished, and he was alone.

To Gregory, as he walked home in the twilight, the whole adventure seemed like a dream, but he made up his mind to try out the wishes on the following day, after first thinking over what he really wanted to make him happy for life.

"This needs careful consideration," he said to himself, "I must not waste a single wish."

He said nothing to anyone at home that evening about what had befallen him, but the others found him unusually silent and thoughtful. When he rose the next morning he had decided that the three things which he wanted most were a fine large house to live in, a beautiful wife, and a money chest that was never empty.

He went straight to the basketmaker and his wife and told them that he was going to the town to seek his fortune and that he would probably never return to the village. His master did not argue with him. "I am sorry to lose you," he said, "you are a good lad and growing skilled at our craft, but you are young and must make your way in the world, and this village is no place for a young man with ambition. You go with my blessing."

And so, after he had said good-by to John and promised to meet him on the steps of the town hall next market day, so that he might relate how he had fared during the week, Gregory set off up the road to the town.

The week passed quickly enough, and on market day John walked to town with his load of baskets for sale. In the afternoon, when he had sold them, he hurried to the town hall to meet Gregory and found him already waiting on the steps. John could hardly recognize his old friend at first, for Gregory was wearing a suit of blue velvet with silver buttons, fine leather boots, and a jaunty velvet cap with a peacock's feather pinned to it by a silver brooch.

"Gregory, what has happened to you? Do not tell me that you have made a fortune already!"

Gregory laughed, delighted at John's surprise, and replied, "Come with me and you will see more than this," and taking him by the arm he led him through the town. They stopped outside a fine house set in a large garden.

"This is my home," said Gregory, and they went inside and were met by a beautiful young woman, dressed in a gown of rich embroidered silk with pearls around her throat. "This is my wife, Isabel," said Gregory. Isabel was as charming as she was lovely, and after she had made the bewildered John welcome she went off to tell the servants that there would be a guest for supper.

While they waited for the meal to be prepared, Gregory told John of his meeting with the Queen of the Woods, and of how he had wished himself a fine house, a beautiful wife, and a money chest that was never empty. "And now I have them," he said, "and I am the happiest fellow in the world."

After supper, which seemed to John like a banquet, he said that he must start for home, and when he had said good-by to Isabel he set off, Gregory saying that he would walk with him as far as the town gates. As they went Gregory said, "Dear John, we have been friends for many years, remember that you will always be welcome at my home, and that if you ever need help I shall always be ready to assist you."

John thanked him, and, as they parted at the gates, Gregory said, "Why not walk home through the wood? You might meet the old woman and her basket of firewood. Only, if you do earn three wishes, make sure you think carefully first and use them wisely as I did."

John walked along the road, still amazed at all that he had seen, and very happy at his friend's good fortune, until he reached the edge of the wood. There he thought, "I might as well try it, though I very much doubt if a simple fellow like myself will ever meet a fairy. Gregory is clever, and such things may well happen to him," and he turned into the wood.

When he was well into the wood he heard a child crying and he saw a little girl holding an empty basket and weeping miserably.

"What ails you, little maid?" he asked.

"Alas, kind sir, my mother sent me into the wood to pick blackberries, and after I had filled my basket I sat down to rest. I fell asleep and when I awoke the birds had eaten all the fruit, and I cannot pick any more, for all that is left is too high for me to reach or too well hidden by the brambles, and if I go home with an empty basket my mother will be angry."

"You need not go home with an empty basket, I will fill it for you," said John. "See, I can reach the blackberries that are high up and I can put my hands through the brambles and reach those that are hidden. But I must work fast, for it will soon be too dark to see them."

And with that he started at once to pick the fruit.

"How lucky that I came into the wood to look for a fairy," he thought. "If I had not I should never have found this little girl, and the poor child might have stayed in the wood all night from fear of her mother."

But as fast as he picked the blackberries, reaching up to the tall brambles above his head and thrusting his hands through the cruel thorns, the basket seemed to fill more slowly than any basket he had ever filled before. To make matters worse, the little girl stood beside him the whole time and scooped handfuls of blackberries out of the basket and ate them with extraordinary speed, saying between each mouthful, "Please hurry, it is growing so dark, and my mother will be wondering where I am."

John longed to tell her to be quiet, and above all, to stop eating any of the blackberries that he had picked with such difficulty, but he thought, "I will not say anything, the poor child must be very hungry, it will be long past her supper time," and he picked on as fast as he could.

At last he had filled the basket, and very tired and scratched John picked up the little girl, set her on his shoulder, and with the basket in his other hand started off through the wood. But it was by now so dark that he found it hard to keep to the path, and he often wandered off it and had to retrace his steps. It seemed to him to be hours later that they reached the edge of the wood.

"We will sit down here and rest a while," he said, "and then you must tell me where you live and I will take you home." The little girl slipped from his shoulder and he put the basket of blackberries down on the grass, but when he turned again to the child she was not there. In her place stood a tall and beautiful lady, whose glimmering robe shone in the dusk. She smiled at him. "I am the Queen of the Woods," she said, "and sometimes it pleases me to seek for a mortal who is kind and patient, so that he may have the reward which he deserves. In return for your kindness to a little girl I give you three wishes. Use them well." And before John could even thank her, she had vanished and he was alone.

John walked home slowly, pondering his good fortune. "I must use the wishes wisely, as Gregory advised," he thought, "though I do not think that I should be happy in a house as large as his. But I should like a little cottage to live in; I think that perhaps I shall use one of my wishes on a cottage. A cottage would be no place for a wife clad in silk and pearls like Isabel, but a simple country maid, such as could love a plain fellow like myself, can be as beautiful as any city lady. I think that I shall use my second wish, like Gregory, on a beautiful wife. A money chest that is never empty may be all very well in a large house with a fine wife, indeed it is probably a necessity, but in a cottage it would only be a responsibility. No, I think that one hundred pieces of gold would be a better sum. That would be plenty for my wife and myself to start our home on. I shall certainly wish for a hundred gold pieces."

Thus John made up his mind how his three wishes could be spent most wisely, and the next day he was still of the same opinion. That evening, when the day's work was over, he went for a stroll through the village toward the fields as he and Gregory had always done since they were boys.

On the outskirts of the village he passed the little cottage where an old widow woman lived alone. She was sitting at her door and he gave her a cheerful "Good evening" and stopped to ask if she wanted any water fetched from the well, for she was so bent with age and infirmity that it was a great task for her to carry a heavy pail of water down her garden path.

After he had drawn the water he stopped and talked a while.

"You are always a good, kind lad to me," said the old woman. "It is so great a joy to me to see a pleasant face. I am so lonely these days, since my son married and went to work in the town. He has asked me to visit him, but I am too old and sick to make the journey and he cannot spare the time from his work to come and see me often. And now I hear that I have a grandson, and what would I not give to be able to see the little darling," and a large tear trickled down her wrinkled cheek.

After he had left her, John said to himself, "I could make that poor old soul happy with one of my wishes, and still have two to spare for myself. After all, I can do without a cottage." And he stopped along the road, closed his eyes tightly, and said out loud and very firmly, "I wish that the old widow woman could grow well and strong so that she might visit her son." Then he thought, "On the way home I shall knock at her door and see if the wish has come true." And with that he jumped over a stile into the fields and walked along whistling.

A little time after, he saw Anna, the miller's youngest daughter, limping slowly toward him carrying a basket of mushrooms. Anna had been lame from birth, she had never been able to run and play like other children, and so had grown up alone, without any friends. Of all the young villagers, only John and Gregory had always been kind and never laughed at her. It was said of her that she would never find a husband, but would live and die an old maid in her father's mill.

"Good evening, Anna. What fine mushrooms you have, I can see you know where to find the best. Is this not a beautiful evening?"

But Anna only looked at him with her large dark eyes and said, "Yes, John, a very beautiful evening," in a sad, tired voice, and went past.

"I do not think she ever smiles," thought John, "and I am sure she never laughs. How ugly it is always to be so sad." And suddenly he remembered the three wishes. "I can give Anna one of my wishes," he thought, "and I shall still have one left for myself. After all, what do I want with a beautiful wife?"

He turned and saw that Anna was clambering awkwardly over the stile with her heavy basket. He closed his eyes and said firmly and out loud—but not so loudly that Anna could hear—"I wish that Anna's foot may grow well and strong, so that she is no longer lame," but when he opened his eyes, Anna was already over the stile and had disappeared along the road behind the hedge.

"I must make a point of keeping a lookout for Anna in the village tomorrow," he decided; "I want to know if the second wish has worked," and he went on across the field singing.

At the farther end of the field was a little thicket, and when he reached it John turned for home, as it was nearing supper time. Just then he heard a whimper of pain from the bushes, and after a search he found a fox with one of its paws caught in a trap.

"This will never do," said John, and he knelt down to unfasten the trap. But try as he might, he could in no way release the spring, and all his efforts only terrified the animal the more, and it struggled so that John was sure that its leg would be torn off if he did not leave it alone.

"But I cannot go away and leave the poor creature here to die," he thought, "and I cannot unfasten the trap, that is certain, so what am I to do?" And then he remembered the last wish. He hesitated only a second, then thought, "After all, now that I am not to have a beautiful wife or a house for her to live in, what need have I of a hundred pieces of gold to marry on?" And closing his eyes tightly, he said out loud and very firmly, "I wish that I might unfasten this trap and free the fox." Then he opened his eyes and made a final attempt and the trap sprang open with ease.

John, well pleased, watched the fox run away through the bushes as fast as three sound legs would carry it, and after snapping the trap shut again, he looked around for a hole to bury it in. He spied one close by, half-hidden by dead leaves, and thrust the trap into it. "You will not catch any more poor animals," he said, but at that moment the iron trap rang against something made of metal which was already in the hole.

John pulled the trap out and felt about in the opening and brought out a small metal box. The lock was rusty and the box opened easily; inside, bright and friendly, were packed shining pieces of gold. John could not believe his eyes. He tipped the gold out on the soft moss and dead leaves and counted it back into the box. There were exactly one hundred pieces.

"Well," said John, "I suppose it is for me," and after he had pushed the trap well into the empty hole and covered the opening with leaves and twigs, he started off again for his supper with the box of gold under his right arm.

When he came to the old widow's cottage, she was standing at her gate waiting for him. "I thought you would pass this way again, John," she said. "I know you will be pleased to hear what I have to tell you. After you had left me this evening a most strange thing happened to me. Suddenly all the pain left my limbs and my body became straight and strong again, and now I feel as fine and well as I have not felt for twenty years or more. To-morrow I shall go to the town to visit my son."

After he had promised to come to see her on the day following her journey to hear all the news, John said good night to her and went on his way.

At the basketmaker's gate he found Anna waiting for him. "Oh, John," she said, "I hope you do not mind my waiting for you, but you have always been kinder to me than the rest, and I had to tell you of my great joy. This evening, after I had passed you, a most strange thing happened to me. Just as I was climbing over the stile, my leg and foot suddenly became well and strong. I could not believe it at first, but when I found that it was true, I ran all the way home with my mushrooms, never stopping once on the way. Oh, John, I am so happy, now that I can walk and run and dance like the other girls."

And John saw that her glad and smiling face was beautiful.

"The day after tomorrow there will be dancing at the forge for the wedding of Matthew, the smith's son. Will you come and dance with me?" he asked, and when she said she would, it was as though all the birds in the village were singing in John's heart.

When the day came, after his work was over John went to the old widow's cottage to see how she had fared. He found her in the highest spirits, and when she had described her visit to the town she told him that she was leaving the village as soon as possible to go and live with her son and his wife.

"And, John," she said, "this little cottage is mine. I would not want it to stand empty and neglected. I have but one son, and as you know, he must live in the town for his trade—for who would buy silverwork in a village? —therefore I should like you to take the cottage as a gift from me, an old woman's way of saying thank you to a kind lad. You may not need it now, but one day you will

marry a wife, and then you will be glad to have a home to take her to."

John could hardly find words with which to thank her, and his good fortune seemed to him to be almost unbelievable.

Later that evening he danced with Anna at the forge and everyone envied him, for Anna was as light as thistledown when she danced, and by far the loveliest girl in the village.

When the dancing was over and they were alone, John said, "Anna, I am only a simple unambitious fellow and I have little to offer you, but I have a cottage where we could live and one hundred gold pieces for us to spend, and I love you more than anything in the world. Will you be my wife?"

And when Anna said "Yes" and smiled at him, it was as though all the birds in the world were singing in John's heart.

"Indeed," he thought, "I am a lucky fellow, for I have had all my three wishes come true without my ever making them."

The Good Sword

Retold by RUTH BRYAN OWEN

FOR many years a shepherd and his son lived on a lonely highland, where they tended the sheep. Their low hut was scarcely higher than the thorny bushes around it. Beyond the grazing place there was a ring of mountains with dark rocks and deep caverns.

The old shepherd always avoided these mountains, and when the sheep wandered near them he made haste to turn them back.

Their life was a hard and lonely one but neither the shepherd nor his son wished to exchange it for any other. Father and son found contentment in each other's company and when the old man fell ill, the boy cared for him tenderly. After a time the old man felt his strength waning and one day he called his son to him and said, "I will soon have to leave you and I grieve that I can give you so small a heritage. Take down the old sword which hangs above our door."

The boy obeyed his father, although the sword felt very heavy in his hand. "This is all I have to give you," said his father. "Always keep it with you and remember that this sword will be victorious in any battle." And giving his son his blessing, the old man closed his eyes and did not open them again.

During the time of his great sorrow, while he was giving his father a proper burial, the son almost forgot about the rusty old sword which had been given to him; but when he closed the hut and drove the sheep down to the distant farm of the owner, the boy strapped the sword to his belt and soon got used to the feel of the heavy weight swinging at his side.

The farmer was surprised to see his flocks coming down from their pastures and bade the boy tell what had befallen his father, and when he had heard, the farmer said, "You are young to have charge of the flock by yourself, but I will let you try it for a while. One thing you must remember—do not let the sheep wander too near to the mountains. There are three pastures lying high on the mountainside which look so brightly green that your beasts may be tempted to clamber up to them, but three trolls live there and each has a small green meadow for himself. If your sheep should wander into one of the trolls' meadows, neither sheep nor shepherd would ever come back again."

The boy thought much of this warning as he drove the flock back toward their grazing place, and as they came nearer to the mountains he kept looking up toward the high green meadows. And in the days that followed, he looked many times toward the trolls' meadows.

Once, when he was tending his sheep, the boy thought suddenly of his sword. "Perhaps a fight with a troll would not be such a bad idea," he said to himself, and he did not drive the sheep back when they wandered toward the mountains. No sooner had the sheep strayed into the small green meadow than a fearful troll came roaring out of his cave. No one who has never seen a wicked troll can picture what an ugly and frightening sight it is.

"Do you know what happens to sheep and shepherds who trespass here?" the troll roared.

"If you mean to harm my sheep, I will have to give you a battle," said the boy, standing his ground.

When he saw how small the boy really was, the troll lashed himself about and breathed out great clouds of smoke. "Now is the time to use my sword," thought the shepherd boy, and as his enemy tried to lay hold of him he brought the sword down on the troll's head with such force that the creature was cut in half by the blow.

The sheep began pulling at the sweet grass of the first troll's meadow and were not content until they had cropped it short. Then they wandered toward the meadow of the second troll. The shepherd boy again did not hinder them and soon a troll far larger and more terrible than the first one came bellowing out of a cavern. "You have not only trespassed on my meadow, which makes your life forfeit, but you have also slain my brother and trampled down his grass."

"If you try to harm me or my sheep I will give you a battle," cried the boy, lifting up his sword.

The troll blew out such clouds of fire and smoke that the boy could scarcely see the frightful creature, but when he brought down his sword the troll was badly cut and died at once.

"Now my sheep have some fresh new grass," said the boy, but while his sheep were eating, he himself entered the third troll's meadow, sword in hand. The troll rushed out of his cavern with such howls of anger that the mountains trembled, but before the monster could say a word the boy rushed forward, crying, "It is your turn now!" and slew him with one blow.

When no troll was left living on the mountain, the boy could not wait to climb down into the great holes where they had lived. The three caverns met together under the earth, and when the shepherd boy came into this cave he saw a red horse with saddle and bridle set with rubies, a red dog which stood by the horse and a suit of crimson armor that lay beside them. Nearby stood a yellow horse with topaz jewels on his harness. A yellow dog and a suit of yellow armor were beside this horse. In another corner of the cave a white horse and a white dog stood near a suit of white armor, and the horse's bridle and the white armor were studded thickly with pearls.

Great chests stood about the cave, filled with coins of silver and gold. It is no wonder that the boy, having slain the trolls and found all this treasure, was in high good spirits, and he went along singing as he drove the sheep back to their fold.

The farmer, who had come to the fold to find out how

it was going with his young shepherd, not only found his sheep safe and bulging with food, but the shepherd boy himself, bubbling over with happiness.

"It is well that you and the flocks are prospering," said the farmer, "but I beg you to stop your singing when all our country is sharing in the King's sadness."

"Why should the King be sad?" asked the boy.

"It is all because of the three dreadful monsters," answered the farmer.

"Not the trolls who lived on our mountain, surely!" said the boy.

"No, it is the three dragons of the sea who are causing all this trouble, and they are larger and more terrible than the trolls on the mountain," said the farmer. "Even the King has no power against them and has finally had to promise that each of his three daughters shall be married to one of them. The King has promised a third of his property to anyone who will rid the kingdom of these dragons. It is said by all that the King is himself without any hope of rescue. It is not proper for you to be singing when everyone else is sorrowful," chided the farmer, as he turned back to his farm.

"The sheep will have to take care of themselves while

I occupy myself with this matter," thought the shepherd, and when the farmer had gone the boy hastened to the cavern of the mountain trolls and put on the red armor and mounted himself on the red horse. Then calling to the red dog to follow him, he rode down to the seashore where the Princesses were to be given to the sea monsters.

In a little while the royal coach came along, and when it had stopped, a Princess stepped out, with a chamberlain beside her. As she stood there, pale with fear, a dragon rose up out of the sea. The chamberlain took one look at its three horrid heads and fled away and hid himself in some thick bushes.

Before the dragon could come near, the trembling Princess saw a horseman on a red horse draw his sword and cut off all three of the dragon's heads. He only stopped to cut the tongues from each of the heads, and rode away again with a red dog following after him.

When he saw that the danger was past, the chamberlain crawled from his hiding place and took charge of everything. "Climb back into the coach," he said to the Princess, "and be sure to let the King know that it was I who saved you. If you do not do this something more dreadful than a dragon will punish you," and the poor Princess, who was not yet over her fear, promised to say nothing at all about the red horseman.

A week later another Princess was to be delivered to the second sea dragon, and this time the shepherd boy put on the yellow armor and mounted the yellow horse, and with the yellow dog following behind him, he rode to the seashore and waited for the second Princess to arrive. Again a dragon came out onto the sands and it was hideous and terrible with six heads, and the chamberlain who had come with the second Princess ran away and hid himself at a safe distance.

The horseman rode forward and slashed the dragon to bits with his sword and then rode away, after he had cut out the dragon's six tongues.

After it was all over, the chamberlain took courage and came back to the Princess, threatening her with dreadful punishment if she should fail to tell the King that it was he himself who had slain the dragon.

"Say nothing about the yellow knight if you value your life," he said, and the second Princess had to do as the chamberlain directed.

When another week had passed, the shepherd boy dressed himself in the white armor and mounted the white

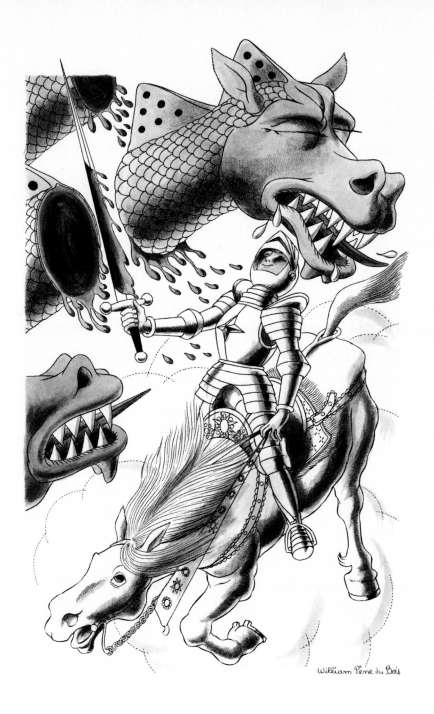

William Pène du Bois

horse, and with the white dog following him, he rode to the beach where the youngest Princess was to be given as a bride to the third sea dragon. This time, the dragon which rose up from the water had nine heads. It is not to be wondered at that the third chamberlain, who had ridden in the royal coach with the youngest Princess, fled away and scrambled up a tree at the first sight of the dreadful creature.

But the Princess, who had been looking all around in the hope that some rescuer would appear, spied the white horseman, and she watched him so intently that she scarcely noticed the dragon until after it had lost all of its nine heads and the white horseman was cutting out its nine tongues, one by one. And because she had not been frightened at the dragon she was only angry when the chamberlain came scurrying back down the tree trunk, and she was not at all ready to listen to him.

"Come here, brave knight," she called to the horseman, and before the chamberlain could notice, she slipped a little gold chain around her rescuer's neck. Then the horseman rode away and the third chamberlain came hurrying with threats of the harm that would come to her if she should fail to name him as her rescuer.

The Good Sword

When the youngest Princess was returned safely to the palace there was great rejoicing, and the three dishonest chamberlains were praised for their courage and promised a rich reward.

"Each of you shall marry the Princess whom he rescued, and have a third of my kingdom," said the King, ordering a holiday and a festival for the Court, and all the people as well.

When the public holiday was proclaimed the shepherd boy asked the farmer if he, too, might take the day for himself.

"Certainly! The King's decree applies even to the humblest," the farmer said, as he gave him leave to join the merrymaking in the village.

Before setting out the shepherd boy called the three dogs from the trolls' cavern, and, followed by a red, a yellow, and a white dog, he came to the village inn. All manner of people were gathered about and there was much talk about the feast which was being given at the castle.

"Wouldn't it be fine to eat some of the good bread they are having there!" exclaimed the innkeeper.

"It would indeed," said the boy, "and it is possible that my dog could find some of the bread for us." So he said to the red dog, "Go to the castle and bring me some of the fine wheat bread they are eating there."

The dog went to the castle, scratched on the doors until they were opened for him and searched about until he found the King's kitchen. Here he seized a loaf of bread in his mouth, and although everyone tried to stop him, the red dog escaped and carried the bread back to the inn and gave it to his master.

After they had eaten the bread, the innkeeper said, "How would it be if we could eat some of the good roast beef from the castle?"

"That is a fine idea," said the boy. "Perhaps my yellow dog will go to the castle and bring some of it for us."

So the yellow dog started out, and when he had reached the castle kitchen he seized a whole roast of beef in his mouth. The cooks tried to stop him, and the kitchen boys chased him with spoons and ladles, but the yellow dog ran back to the inn and gave the beef to his master.

The next day, when the weddings were to take place, the innkeeper said, "How wonderful it would be to have a sip of wine from the King's table!"

"That would be a good idea," said the boy. "Surely my white dog could fetch a bottle of wine for us."

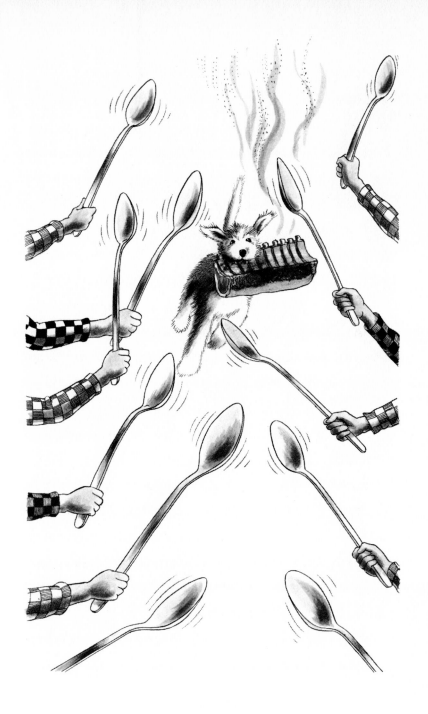

When he commanded, the white dog went to the castle and into the hall where all the wedding guests were seated at the King's table, and, before any one of the amazed guests could say a word, it snatched a bottle of wine and ran with it to the inn. When the youngest Princess saw the white dog she clapped her hands and cried, "It was that white dog's master who saved me from the dragon!"

"What nonsense is this?" her bridegroom cried, angrily. "You know quite well that it was I who saved you."

"You have tried to make it appear so," said the Princess, "but now that I see the white dog, I know his master must be near. If you persist in your wicked stories he will serve you as he served the dragon. I will follow the white dog until I find my rescuer," and the Princess jumped up from the table.

"Let us all follow the dog," cried the King, and he and all the lords and ladies of the Court rushed out, too, and followed the dog to the inn. The shepherd boy was much astonished to see all the crowd and wanted to hide himself, but the youngest Princess cried, "My golden chain will be found around the neck of the man who killed the dragon," and the shepherd boy showed the golden chain which he had under his shirt.

The Good Sword

But the third chamberlain began to shout, "Ho! Ho! how can this boy pretend that he has slain the dragon when I have the proof that I did it," and he brought in the nine heads of the last dragon which had been killed.

"My rescuer took the tongues from the dragon's heads," said the Princess, and the shepherd boy showed them not only the nine tongues which he had cut from this dragon's heads, but also the tongues from the heads of the other two dragons, so that no one could be in doubt about the matter any longer.

The three chamberlains were led away in disgrace to receive punishment for their crimes, and the shepherd boy set off for the castle, hand in hand with the youngest Princess, to whom he was married amid great rejoicing.

But he did not forget how much he owed to the good sword, and he had it hung up in a place of honor, for even a King feels a little more secure when he has a sword which can be trusted to win every battle for him.

Where to Lay the Blame

by HOWARD PYLE

THERE was once upon a time a fisherman who had fished all day long and had caught not so much as a sprat. So at night there he sat by the fire, rubbing his knees and warming his shins, and waiting for supper that his wife was cooking for him. His hunger was as sharp as vinegar, and his temper hot enough to fry fat.

While he sat there grumbling and growling and trying to make himself comfortable and warm, there suddenly came a knock at the door. The good woman opened it, and there stood an old man, clad all in red from head to foot, and with a snowy beard at his chin as white as winter snow.

The fisherman's wife stood gaping and staring at the strange figure, but the old man in red walked straight into the hut. "Bring your nets, fisherman," said he, "and come with me. There is something that I want you to catch for me, and if I have luck I will pay you for your fishing as never fisherman was paid before."

"Not I," said the fisherman; "I go out no more this night. I have been fishing all day long until my back is nearly broken, and have caught nothing, and now I am not such a fool as to go out and leave a warm fire and a good supper at your bidding."

But the fisherman's wife had listened to what the old man had said about paying for the job, and she was of a different mind from her husband. "Come," said she, "the old man promises to pay you well. This is not a chance to be lost, and my advice to you is that you go."

The fisherman shook his head. No, he would not go; he had said he would not, and he would not. But the wife only smiled and said again, "My advice to you is that you go."

The fisherman grumbled and grumbled, and swore that he would not go. The wife said nothing but one thing. She did not argue; she did not lose her temper; she only said to everything that he said, "My advice to you is that you go."

At last the fisherman's anger boiled over. "Very well," said he, spitting his words at her; "if you will drive me out into the night, I suppose I will have to go." And then he spoke the words that so many men say: "Many a man has come to trouble by following his wife's advice."

Down he took his fur cap and up he took his nets, and off he and the old man marched through the moonlight, their shadows bobbing along like black spiders behind them.

Well, on they went, out from the town and across the fields and through the woods, until at last they came to a dreary, lonesome desert, where nothing was to be seen but gray rocks and weeds and thistles.

"Well," said the fisherman, "I have fished, man and boy, for forty-seven years, but never did I see as unlikely a place to catch anything as this."

But the old man said never a word. First of all he drew a great circle with strange figures, marking it with his finger upon the ground. Then out from under his red gown he brought a tinderbox and steel, and a little silver casket covered all over with strange figures of serpents and dragons and what not. He brought some sticks of spicewood from his pouch, and then he struck a light and made a fire. Out of the box he took a gray powder, which he flung upon the little blaze.

Puff! flash! A vivid flame went up into the moonlight, and then a dense smoke as black as ink, which spread out wider and wider, far and near, till all below was darker than the darkest midnight. The old man began to utter strange spells and words. Presently there began a rumbling that sounded louder and louder and nearer and nearer, until it roared and bellowed like thunder. The earth rocked and swayed, and the poor fisherman shook and trembled with fear till his teeth chattered in his head.

Suddenly the roaring and bellowing ceased, and all was as still as death, though the darkness was as thick and black as ever.

"Now," said the old magician—for such he was—"now we are about to take a journey such as no one ever traveled before. Heed well what I tell you. Speak not a single word, for if you do, misfortune will be sure to happen to you."

"Ain't I to say anything?" said the fisherman.

"No."

"Not even 'boo' to a goose?"

"No."

"Well, that is pretty hard upon a man who likes to say his say," said the fisherman.

"And moreover," said the old man, "I must blindfold you as well."

Thereupon he took from his pocket a handkerchief, and made ready to tie it about the fisherman's eyes.

"And ain't I to see anything at all?" said the fisherman.

"No."

"Not even so much as a single feather?"

"No."

"Well, then," said the fisherman, "I wish I'd not come."

But the old man tied the handkerchief tightly around his eyes, and he was as blind as a bat.

"Now," said the old man, "throw your leg over what you feel and hold fast."

The fisherman reached down his hand, and there felt the back of something rough and hairy. He flung his leg over it, and whisk! whizz! off he shot through the air like a skyrocket. Nothing was left for him to do but grip tightly with hands and feet and to hold fast. On they went, and on they went, until, after a great while, whatever it was that was carrying him lit upon the ground, and there the fisherman found himself standing.

That which had brought him had gone.

The old man whipped the handkerchief off his eyes and saw that he was on the shores of the sea, where there was nothing to be seen but water upon one side and rocks and naked sand upon the other.

"This is the place for you to cast your nets," said the old magician, "for if we catch nothing here we catch nothing at all."

The fisherman unrolled his nets and cast them and dragged them, and then cast them and dragged them again. Neither time did he catch so much as a herring. But the third time that he cast he found that he had caught something that weighed as heavy as lead. He pulled and pulled, until by and by he dragged the load ashore. What should it be but a great chest of wood, blackened by the sea water, and covered with shells and green moss.

That was the very thing that the magician had come to fish for.

From his pouch the old man took a little golden key, which he fitted into a keyhole in the side of the chest. He threw back the lid; the fisherman looked within, and there was the prettiest little palace that man's eye ever

beheld, all made of mother-of-pearl and silver-frosted as white as snow. The old magician lifted the little palace out of the box and set it upon the ground.

Then, lo and behold! a marvelous thing happened; for the palace instantly began to grow for all the world like a soap bubble, until it stood in the moonlight gleaming and glistening like snow, the windows bright with the lights of a thousand wax tapers, and the sound of music and voices and laughter coming from within.

Hardly could the fisherman catch his breath from one strange thing when another happened. The old magician took off his clothes and his face—yes, his face—for all the world as though it had been a mask, and there stood as handsome and noble a young man as ever the light looked on. Beckoning to the fisherman—who was dumb with wonder—he led the way up the great flight of marble steps to the palace door.

As he came the door swung open with a blaze of light, and there stood hundreds of noblemen, all clad in silks and satins and velvets, who, when they saw the magician, bowed low before him, as though he had been a king. Leading the way, they brought the two through halls and chambers and room after room, each more magnificent than the other, until they came to one that surpassed a hundredfold any of the others.

At the farther end was a golden throne, and upon it sat a lady more lovely and beautiful than a dream, her eyes as bright as diamonds, her cheeks like rose leaves, and her hair like spun gold. She came halfway down the steps of the throne to welcome the magician, and when the two met they kissed one another before all those who were looking on. Then she brought him to the throne and seated him beside her, and there they talked for a long time very earnestly.

Nobody said a word to the fisherman, who stood staring about him like an owl. "I wonder," said he to himself at last, "if they will give a body a bite to eat by and by?" for, to tell the truth, the good supper that he had come away from at home had left a sharp hunger gnawing at his insides, and he longed for something good and warm to fill the empty place. But time passed, and not so much as a crust of bread was brought to stay his stomach.

Soon the clock struck twelve, and then the two who sat upon the throne arose. The beautiful lady took the magician by the hand, and, turning to those who stood around, said, in a loud voice, "Behold him who alone is worthy to possess the jewel of jewels! Unto him do I give it, and with it all power of powers!" Thereon she opened a golden casket that stood beside her, and brought thence a little crystal ball, about as big as a pigeon's egg, in which was something that glistened like a spark of fire. The magician took the crystal ball and thrust it into his bosom;

but what it was the fisherman could not guess, and if you do not know I shall not tell you.

Then for the first time the beautiful lady seemed to notice the fisherman. She beckoned him, and when he stood beside her two men came carrying a chest. The chief treasurer opened it, and it was full of bags of gold money. "How will you have it?" said the beautiful lady.

"Have what?" said the fisherman.

"Have the pay for your labor?" said the beautiful lady.

"I will," said the fisherman, promptly, "take it in my hat."

"So be it," said the beautiful lady. She waved her hand, and the chief treasurer took a bag from the chest, untied it, and emptied a cataract of gold into the fur cap. The fisherman had never seen so much wealth in all his life before, and he stood like a man turned to stone.

"Is all this mine?" said the fisherman.

"It is," said the beautiful lady.

"Then God bless your pretty eyes," said the fisherman.

The magician kissed the beautiful lady, and, beckoning to the fisherman, left the throne room the same way that they had come. The noblemen, in silks and satins and velvets, marched ahead, and back they went through the other apartments, until at last they came to the door. Out they stepped, and then what do you suppose happened?

If the wonderful palace had grown like a bubble, like a bubble it vanished. There the two stood on the seashore, with nothing to be seen but rocks and sand and water, and the starry sky overhead.

The fisherman shook his cap of gold, and it jingled and tinkled, and was as heavy as lead. If it was not all a dream, he was rich for life.

"But anyhow," said he, "they might have given a body a bite to eat."

The magician put on his red clothes and his face again, making himself as hoary and as old as before. He took out his flint and steel, and his sticks of spicewood and his gray powder, and made a great fire and smoke just as he had done before. Then again he tied his handkerchief over the fisherman's eyes.

"Remember," said he, "what I told you when we started upon our journey. Keep your mouth tight shut, for if you utter so much as a single word you are a lost man. Now throw your leg over what you feel and hold fast."

The fisherman had his net over one arm and his cap of gold in the other hand; nevertheless, there he felt the same hairy thing he had felt before. He flung his leg over it, and away he was gone through the air like a rocket.

Now, he had grown somewhat used to strange things by this time, so he began to think that he would like to see what sort of creature it was upon which he was riding thus through the sky. So he contrived, in spite of his net and cap, to push up the handkerchief from over one eye. Out he peeped, and then he saw as clear as day what the strange steed was.

He was riding upon a he-goat as black as night, and in front of him was the magician riding upon just such another, his great red robe fluttering out behind him in the moonlight like huge red wings.

"Great herring and little fishes!" roared the fisherman, "it's a billy goat!"

Instantly goats, old man, and all were gone like a flash. Down fell the fisherman through the empty sky, whirling over and over and around and around like a frog. He held tightly to his net, but away flew his fur cap, the golden money falling in a shower like sparks of yellow light. Down he fell and down he fell, until his head spun like a top.

By good luck his house was just below, with its thatch of soft rushes. Into the very middle of it he tumbled, and right through the thatch—bump!—into the room below.

The good wife was in bed, snoring away for dear life, but such a noise as the fisherman made coming into the house was enough to wake the dead. Up she jumped, and there she sat, staring and winking with sleep, and with her brains as addled as a duck's egg in a thunderstorm.

"There!" said the fisherman, as he gathered himself up and rubbed his shoulder, "that is what comes of following a woman's advice!"

The Story of Wang Li

by ELIZABETH COATSWORTH

ONCE in China many many years ago there lived a young man named Wang Li, with his old mother, on a small farm under the shadow of the Hill of the Seven Stars. When he was a boy he studied letters and charms with a famous sage who lived by himself in the Wind Cave halfway up the mountain. But when he had studied for several years he declared one morning that he would climb the rough path no more.

His mother was in despair.

"How hard have I labored without your help in the fields!" she cried. "Why, in a few years you could have called the cranes out of the sky to carry us anywhere we wished, or turned flower petals into money to buy whatever we desired! Ungrateful son! Return to your studies!"

But Wang Li only shook his head.

"I have learned all that I need," he replied. *"A big heart is better than a big house."*

Upon hearing a proverb quoted at her, Wang Li's mother grew furious, and seizing her broom, beat Wang Li over the shoulders until she was tired. He, being a filial son in most matters, waited until she had stopped, and then brought her a drink of cold water fresh from the well.

After that Wang Li helped his mother in the fields, but often he slipped away to the forests at the foot of the Hill of the Seven Stars with his bow and arrow, to wander in their green shades and perhaps bring back a hare for their dinner, until he became as expert a hunter as there was in the countryside.

So the days went by and at last there came a dry spring. Week after week passed and still no rain fell and the young rice and millet shoots stood small and yellow in the fields, and the mulberry leaves hung withered on the trees, unfit for the silkworms, and the melon vines lay brittle as straws on the baked ground. Prayers were said all day long in the Temple of the God of the Soil. Incense burned in great twisted ropes of sweetness about his nostrils, gongs were sounded before him, and offerings of fish and chickens and pork lay heaped on his altars.

But still no rain fell.

Early one morning Wang Li was wandering in the forest when he saw something above his head that looked like a flight of great swans, slowly settling down towards the clear waters of Heaven Mirror Lake. Creeping without sound through the underbrush, he at last came to a thicket at the very edge of the water, and parting the leaves with careful hands, he beheld a most beautiful sight. The creatures whom he had seen were not swans but winged maidens who were playing about on the surface, splashing the water until it shone like the crystal beads in their elaborate headdresses, shaking their white wings with a sound like music, clapping their delicate hands, and pursuing one another in sport.

It happened that during their games the most beautiful of the damsels passed close to the thicket where Wang Li was hidden. Swift as a hawk he seized one snow-white wing in his strong hand, and while the other maidens rose screaming into the air, he drew his lovely captive to the shore.

For a little while she wept, but glancing at him through

[*213*]

her lashes, she was reassured and ceased to sob. Still holding the edge of one bright wing, he questioned her.

"What is your name, beautiful one?" he asked.

"I am called the Sky Damsel and am the youngest daughter of the Cloud Dragon," she answered timidly. And then went on: "You are the first human being I have ever seen. If you will come with me I will take you to the sixteen palaces of my father that are built upon the clouds. One palace is of white jade and silver, and butterflies guard the gates; another palace is built of marble inlaid with rose quartz, and its gardens are famous for their peonies; another palace has walls of gold, and is overlooked by a high pagoda on which stands the bird of the sun to crow to the dawn; and the last palace is built of ebony with pavilions of scarlet lacquer, and Lightning stands on the left of the gate and Thunder on the right. If you will come, you shall be my husband and live in whichever palace you please, and you shall ride on steeds of vapor and pluck the stars as you pass."

"I am a poor man," said Wang Li, "and the son of a poor man. How should I live in a palace? But if I give you your freedom, Sky Damsel, will you swear to me that in return you will ask your august parent to send upon this unfortunate countryside the requisite rains, so that the crops shall flourish and the people may not die? And he might keep a special eye on my mother's little farm at the foot of Seven Stars Hill," he added, "for she works hard and likes her garden to do well."

"It shall be as you have said," replied the Sky Damsel, and she flew away, often looking back and weeping.

But Wang Li returned home, and as he neared his mother's house the rain began to fall, soft and warm, filling all the ditches with the gurgle of running water.

"Rejoice," cried his mother as he entered, "the drought is over! And just in time, too! Now the crops will be spared. I wonder how it occurred?"

"Oh, I know all about *that*," said Wang Li, and he told her what had happened by the lonely shore of Heaven Mirror Lake.

At once his mother flew into a rage.

"And you only asked for rain," she screamed, "when we might have lived in palaces, and worn silk woven from moonlight, and fed on the fruit of the immortals! Oh, you undutiful son!"

And she fell to beating him with her broom. But when at last she stopped exhausted, he only remarked:

"A chicken coop is still a chicken coop even when covered with cloth of gold." And he lifted a pot of dumplings which was in danger of boiling over.

Now the next year it happened that Roving Horse River was in flood, spreading out over its banks, ruining fields, and carrying away houses. Its waters came up nearly to the door of the cottage where Wang Li and his mother lived, and threatened her mulberry trees. She was in despair and wept bitterly, but Wang Li took his bow and arrow from the wall.

"Are you going hunting at such a time?" she screamed. "Oh, that I should have borne a son with no heart!"

But he only said: *"If you know how, a thing is not hard; if it is hard, then you don't know how."* And he left her with her mouth open, not understanding what he meant.

"I wish that boy would stop quoting proverbs," she muttered to herself. "He is as clever a boy as ever breathed, but what good does it do us?"

Meantime Wang Li walked along beside the bank of the river. And he saw the flood coming down in a great white wave. And having very keen eyes he saw in the midst of the wave a youth and a maiden, clothed in garments of white silk, riding white horses with silver bits. And attendants on white horses followed them.

Then Wang Li drew his bow, fitted an arrow into the string, and let it fly straight into the heart of the young man, who fell dead from his horse. At that the others turned their horses and rode away at full speed, and the flood receded with them.

But as they rode, Wang Li sent another arrow after them, which pierced the high headdress of the noble lady and shone there like a long ornament. And after a few paces, she reined in her horse and slowly rode back to where Wang Li stood.

"Here is your arrow," she said, giving it to him. "I suppose I should thank you for not sending it through my heart as you did through my cousin's, the Prince of Roving Horse River."

"I could never do anything so discourteous," murmured Wang Li.

The lady regarded him for a long time.

"Since you have spared my person," she said, "I suppose it should be yours. If you will come with me you shall be my husband, and reign in the palaces of the River Dragons. You shall sit on a throne of coral in halls of

jade and crystal, and the River Maidens shall dance before you the Dance of the Ripples, and the River Warriors
shall dance to please you the Dance of the Tempest."

"And what will happen to the countryside while they
dance?" asked Wang Li. "No, no, I am a poor man and
the son of a poor man. What should I do in palaces? If
you wish to show your gratitude, make me a pledge that
the river shall hereafter stay within its banks, and perhaps you might be especially careful along the edge of my
mother's farm, for she is a poor woman and it grieves her
to see her work washed away."

The lady raised her hand in agreement, and turned her
horse, and rode off. But before she disappeared forever,
she looked back for a last glimpse of Wang Li, and he
saw that she was weeping. A little sad, he returned to his
mother's house and, as he walked, he noticed how the
waters were draining off the land, leaving behind them,
as tribute, pools filled with round-mouthed fish.

His mother met him at the door.

"See! see!" she cried, "the waters are withdrawing! But
you, you wicked son, you left me here to drown and little
you cared!"

"Indeed, I only went to bring you help!" said Wang Li,

and he told his mother all that had happened. At hearing the story she nearly choked with rage.

"What! We might have lived in river palaces and dined off turtle eggs and carps' tongues every day!" she cried. "And I might have ridden on a dragon forty feet long when I went calling! All this might have been mine but you refused it, you ungrateful son!" And she seized her broom.

Whack!

"Take that!"

Whack!

"And that!"

Whack! Whack! Whack!

"And that! and that! and that!"

But when at last her arm fell, Wang Li politely helped her to her chair and brought her a fan.

"Peace in a thatched hut—that is happiness," he said, once more quoting an old proverb.

"Be off with you!" replied his mother. "You are a wicked, ungrateful son and have no right to be using the words of wise men. Besides, they hadn't been offered palaces, I'm sure."

So the months passed and the rain fell when it was

needed, and the river remained within its banks and re-
flected on its smooth waters the sun by day and the moon
by night. But after some time the country was greatly dis-
turbed by earthquakes. People were awakened from their
sleep by the tremblings of their beds, the dishes danced
on the tables, sheds fell flat to the earth, and everyone
waited with horror for the final quake that should bring
their roofs down about their heads.

"Now," wept Wang Li's old mother, "I shall die a
violent death, I who might have slept safe beside the
Silver Stream of Heaven or walked in the gardens of the
river, if it had not been for this great foolish son."

But Wang Li took his spear and went to the mouth of
the Cave of the Evening Sun which is on the west side
of the Hill of the Seven Stars. Then he looked carefully
at the ground beneath his feet, which was rounded up as
though a huge mole had passed under it, and choosing
a certain spot, drove his spear deep into the loosened soil.

"Whoever walks along that path again will scratch his
back," he said to himself with satisfaction, and was about
to return home when he noticed a beautiful girl who sat
beside a rock spinning, and weeping as she spun.

"Why do you scatter the pearls of your eyes, young

maiden?" asked Wang Li gently. And she, raising her tear-wet eyes to him, said:

"Alas, I am Precious Jade, the only daughter of the former Dragon King of the Mountains. But my ungrateful uncle has risen against his elder brother and imprisoned him in the innermost prison of the hills, and he has driven me out to work with unaccustomed hands, living in this coarse robe, and eating roots and berries, and sleeping under the stars."

Wang Li looked at her in her rough brown garments, and her beauty seemed like a flower bursting from its sheath.

"I think I have stopped the path of your uncle who has been disturbing us with his wanderings, and now perhaps he will stay in his cavern palaces. But for you I can do nothing, I fear, though I would gladly serve you."

At that Precious Jade looked at him shyly.

"If you would deign to take me away with you and allow me to serve your mother with my poor strength, I should no longer weep alone on this desolate mountain," she whispered.

"And what gifts would you bring my mother if I took you home as a bride?" asked Wang Li.

Then Precious Jade wrung her hands. "Alas," she said, "I have no gifts but only my will to serve you both." And she wept very bitterly.

At that Wang Li laughed and lifted her up in his arms and carried her home to his mother.

"Mercy!" cried the old woman, "whom have we here?"

"It is Precious Jade, the daughter of the former Dragon King of the Mountains," said Wang Li, "and she has returned here to be your daughter-in-law."

The old woman was all in a flutter.

"I must have an hour to get ready before I can present myself at court. How many guests will there be at the feast, my little dove? And how many rooms shall I have in the palace? And what color are the lanterns, or does light shine from the gems themselves in the Kingdom of the Mountain Dragons?"

"Alas!" said Precious Jade, "my father is a prisoner and I am only an exile."

"Pshaw!" exclaimed the old woman, "what a daughter-in-law for you to bring back, you senseless oaf! Look at the robe she is wearing, and her hands are fit for nothing! Go and bring me a pail of water, you useless girl! As for you," she cried, turning to her son, "you shall feel if my old arms are withered yet!" And she caught up her broom and began belaboring him with it.

"*A thin horse has long hair,*" remarked Wang Li philosophically when she had done, and he went out into the garden to find her a peach to refresh her after so much effort.

"I shall have to make the best of it," she grumbled to herself, when she had eaten the peach. "The boy has ears of stone. He follows his own way. If the mountain will not turn, I must be the road and do the turning myself." After that she was kind to Precious Jade, who tried to be of help to her mother-in-law in every possible way.

So they lived together in peace and happiness, working hard, incurring no debts and showing kindness to all. Throughout the district the rains fell punctually, no one had any complaint of Roving Horse River, and the earth was no longer shaken by the burrowing of dragons. In time Precious Jade bore a beautiful son whom they named Little Splendor and there were never four happier people in the world. One day, not long afterwards, as Wang Li and Precious Jade sat alone beneath a grapevine trellis which Wang Li had recently made, Precious Jade began, laying down her embroidery:

"My dear husband, a message has reached me from my father. It seems that my unworthy uncle, issuing forth hastily from his palace, struck himself against the point of your spear and after some time died. My father is again on his jewel throne, and naturally feels a deep gratitude towards you." She paused.

"Now you are going to tell me about the palaces under the mountains which I may have for the asking," said Wang Li.

"I always hated palaces. There was never anything to do," said Precious Jade, smiling. Then she went back to her embroidery.

"My husband is the proudest man in the world," she remarked to a yellow silk butterfly which she had not quite finished.

"Proud?" asked Wang Li, "yet here I am and I might be a prince."

"You're too proud to be a prince," she replied, "and that is why I love you. I always wanted to marry the proudest man in the world."

"Maybe it's pride and maybe it's wisdom," said Wang Li, "but there are palaces and terraces of the mind I would not exchange for all the riches of the dragons."

And Precious Jade understood. In time Wang Li became so famous for his wisdom and benevolence that sages traveled from the farthest provinces to walk with him as he followed his plow. But sometimes when he was busy and the old mother needed a new silk gown or the baby wanted sweetmeats, Precious Jade would softly shake the leaves of the tree beside the door, and down would fall a light shower of silver coins. And Wang Li never noticed what it was that Precious Jade gathered under the mulberry tree.

Casperl

by HENRY C. BUNNER

CASPERL was a wood chopper, and the son of a wood chopper, and although he was only eighteen when his father died, he was so strong and active that he went on chopping and hauling wood for the whole neighborhood. People said he did it quite as well as his father, while he was certainly a great deal more pleasant in his manner and much more willing to oblige others.

It was a poor country, however, for it was right in the heart of the Black Forest, and there were more witches and fairies and goblins there than healthy human beings. So Casperl scarcely made a living although he worked hard and rose early in the morning, summer and winter. His friends often advised him to go to some better place, where he could earn more money. But he only shook his head and said that the place was good enough for him.

He never told anyone, though, why he loved his poor hut in the depths of the dark forest, because it was a secret which he did not wish to share with strangers. For he had discovered, a mile or two from his home, in the very blackest part of the woods, an enchanted mountain. It was a high mountain, covered with trees and rocks and thick, tangled undergrowth, except at the very top, where there stood a castle surrounded by smooth green lawns and beautiful gardens. They were always kept in the neatest possible order, although no gardener was ever seen.

This enchanted mountain had been under a spell for nearly two hundred years. The lovely Princess who lived there had once ruled the whole country. But a powerful and wicked magician disguised himself as a prince, and made love to her. At first the Princess loved her false suitor; but one day she found out that he was not what he pretended to be, and she told him to leave her and never to come near her again.

"For you are not a prince," she said. "You are an impostor, and I will never wed any but a true prince."

"Very well," said the magician, in a rage. "You shall

wait for your true prince, if there is such a thing as a true prince; and you shall marry no one till he comes."

And then the magician cast a spell upon the beautiful castle on the top of the mountain, and the terrible forest sprang up about it. Rocks rose up out of the earth and piled themselves in great heaps among the tree trunks. Saplings and brush and twisted poisonous vines came to fill up every crack and crevice, so that no mortal man could possibly go to the summit, except by one path, which was purposely left clear. And in that path there was a gate that the strongest man could not open, it was so heavy. Farther up the mountain slope, the trunk of a tree lay right across the way—a magic tree, that no one could climb over or crawl under or cut through. And beyond the gate and the tree was a dragon with green eyes that frightened away every man that looked at it.

And there the beautiful Princess was doomed to live until the true prince should arrive and overcome these three obstacles.

Now, although none of the people in the forest, except Casperl, knew of the mountain or the Princess, the story had been told in many distant countries, and year after year young princes came from all parts of the earth to try to rescue the lovely captive and win her for a bride. But, one after the other, they all tried and failed. The best of them could not so much as open the gate.

And so there the Princess remained, as the years went on. But she did not grow any older, or any less beautiful, for she was still waiting for the True Prince, and she believed that some day he would come.

This was what kept Casperl from leaving the Black Forest. He was sorry for the Princess, and he hoped some day to see her rescued and wedded to the True Prince.

Every evening, when his work was done, he would walk to the foot of the mountain, and sit down on a great stone, and look up to the top where the Princess was walking in her garden. And as it was an enchanted mountain, he could see her clearly, although she was so far away. Yes, he could see her face as well as though she were close by him, and he thought it was truly the loveliest face in the world.

There he would sit and sadly watch the princes who tried to climb the hill. There was scarcely a day that some prince from a far country did not come to make the attempt. One after another, they would arrive with gorgeous trains of followers, mounted on fine horses, and dressed in costumes so magnificent that a plain cloth-of-gold suit looked shabby among them. They would look up to the mountaintop and see the Princess walking there, and they would praise her beauty so warmly that Casperl, when he heard them, felt sure he was quite right in thinking her the loveliest woman in the world.

But every prince had to make the trial by himself. That was one of the conditions which the magician made when he laid the spell upon the castle, although Casperl did not know it.

And each prince would throw off his cloak, and shoulder a silver or gold-handled ax, and fasten his sword by his side, and set out to climb the hill, and open the gate, and cut through the fallen tree, and slay the dragon, and wed the Princess.

Up he would go, bright and hopeful, and tug away at the gate until he found that he could do nothing with it, and then he would plunge into the tangled thickets of underbrush, and try his best to fight his way through to the summit.

But every one of them came back, after a while, with his fine clothes torn and his soft skin scratched, all tired and disheartened and worn out. And then he would look spitefully up at the mountain, and say he didn't care so much about wedding the Princess, after all; that she was only a common enchanted princess, just like any other enchanted princess, and really not worth so much trouble.

This would grieve Casperl, for he couldn't help thinking that it was impossible that any other woman could be as lovely as *his* Princess. You see, he called her *his* Princess because he took such an interest in her, and he didn't think there could be any harm in speaking of her in that way, just to himself. For he never supposed she could even know that there was such a humble creature as poor young Casperl, the wood chopper, who sat at the foot of the hill and looked up at her.

And so the days went on, and the unlucky princes came and went, and Casperl watched them all. Sometimes he saw his Princess look down from over the castle parapets, and eagerly follow with her lovely eyes the struggles of some brave suitor through the thickets, until the poor prince gave up the job in despair. Then she would look sad and turn away. But generally she paid no attention to the attempts that were being made to reach her. That kind of thing had been going on so long that she was quite used to it.

By and by, one summer evening, as Casperl sat watching, there came a Prince with a small train of attendants. The Prince was rather undersized; he didn't look strong, and he *did* look as though he slept too much in the morning and too little at night. He slipped off his cloak, however, and climbed up the road, and began to push and pull at the gate.

Casperl watched him carelessly for a while, and then, happening to look up, he saw that the Princess was gazing sadly down on the poor little Prince as he tugged and toiled.

A bold idea came to Casperl. Why shouldn't he help the Prince? He was young and strong; he had often thought that, if he were a prince, a gate like that should not keep him away from the Princess. Why should he not give his strength to help free her?

So he walked modestly up the hill and offered his services to the Prince.

"Your Royal Highness," he said, "I am only a wood chopper; but, if you please, I am a strong wood chopper, and perhaps I can be of use to you."

"But why should you take the trouble to help me?" inquired the Prince. "What good will it do you?"

"Oh, well!" said Casperl, "it's helping the Princess, too, don't you know?"

"No, I don't know," said the Prince. "However, you may try what you can do. Here, put your shoulder to this end of the gate, and I will stand right behind you."

Now, Casperl did not know that it was forbidden to any suitor to have help in his attempt to climb the hill. The Prince knew it, though, but he said to himself, "When I am through with this wood chopper I will dismiss him, and no one will know anything about it. I can never lift this gate by myself. I will let him do it for me, and thus I shall get the Princess, and he will be just as well satisfied, for he is only a wood chopper."

So Casperl put his broad shoulder to the gate and pushed with all his might. It was very heavy, but after a while it began to move a little.

"Courage, your Royal Highness!" said Casperl. "We'll move it, after all." But if he had looked over his shoulder, he would have seen that the little Prince was not pushing at all. He had put on his cloak, and was standing idly by, laughing to himself at the way he was making a wood chopper do his work for him.

After a long struggle, the gate gave way, and swung

open just wide enough to let them through. It was a close squeeze for the Prince; but Casperl held the gate open until he slipped through.

"Dear me," said the Prince, "you're quite a strong fellow. You really were of some assistance to me. Let me see, I think the stories say something about a tree, or some such thing, farther up the road. As you are a wood chopper, and as you have your ax with you, perhaps you might walk up a bit and see if you can't make yourself useful."

Casperl was quite willing, for he began to feel that he was doing something for the Princess, and it pleased him to think that even a wood chopper could do her a service.

So they walked up until they came to the tree. And then the Prince drew out his silver ax, and sharpened it carefully on the sole of his shoe, while Casperl picked up a stone and whetted his old iron ax, which was all he had.

"Now," said the Prince, "let's see what we can do."

But he really didn't do anything. It was Casperl who swung his ax and chopped hard at the magic tree. Every blow made the chips fly; but the wood grew instantly over every cut, just as though he had been cutting into water.

For a while the Prince amused himself by trying first

to climb over the tree, and then to crawl under it. But he soon found that whichever way he went, the tree grew up or down so fast that he was shut off. Finally he gave it up, and went back and lay down on his back on the grass, and watched Casperl working.

And Casperl worked hard. The tree grew fast; but he chopped faster. His forehead was wet and his arms were tired, but he worked away and made the chips fly in a cloud. He was too busy to take the time to look over his shoulder, so he did not see the Prince lying on the grass. But every now and then he spoke cheerily, saying, "We'll do it, your Royal Highness!"

And he did it. In the end, after a long, long while, he got the better of the magic tree, for he chopped quicker than it could grow, and at last he had cut a gap right across the trunk.

The Prince jumped up from the grass and leaped nimbly through, and Casperl followed him slowly and sadly, for he was tired and it began to occur to him that the Prince hadn't said anything about the Princess. That made him wonder if the little man who called himself Prince were the True Prince, after all. "I'm afraid," thought Casperl, "that the Princess won't thank me if I bring her a prince who doesn't love her. And it really is very strange that this Prince hasn't said a word about her."

So he ventured to remark, very meekly, "Your Royal Highness will be glad to see the Princess?"

"Oh, no doubt," replied the Prince.

"And the Princess will be very glad to see your Royal Highness," went on Casperl.

"Oh, of course!" said the Prince.

"And your Royal Highness will be very good to the Princess," said Casperl further, by way of a hint.

"I think," said the Prince, "that you are talking altogether too much about the Princess. I don't believe I need you any more. Perhaps you had better go home. I'm much obliged to you for your assistance. I can't reward you just now, but if you will come to see me after I have married the Princess, I may be able to do something for you."

Casperl turned away, somewhat disappointed, and was going down the hill, when the Prince called him back.

"Oh, by the way!" he said, "there's a dragon, I understand, a little farther on. Perhaps you'd like to come along and see me kill him?"

Casperl thought he would like to see the Prince do something for the Princess, so he followed him. Very

soon they came to the top of the mountain, and saw the green lawns and beautiful gardens of the enchanted castle —and there was the dragon waiting for them.

The dragon reared itself on its dreadful tail, and flapped its black wings; its great green, shining, scaly body swelled and twisted, and it roared in a terrible way.

The little Prince drew his jeweled sword and walked slowly up to the monster. And then the great beast opened its red mouth and blew out one awful breath, that caught the Prince up as if he were a feather, and whisked him clear off the mountain and over the tops of the trees in the valley.

And that was the last anyone ever saw of him!

Then Casperl grasped his old ax and leaped forward to meet the dragon, never stopping to think how poor his weapon was. But all of a sudden the dragon vanished and disappeared and was gone, and there was no trace of it anywhere; but the beautiful Princess stood in its place and smiled and held out her white hand to Casperl.

"My Prince!" she said. "So you have come at last!"

"I beg your gracious Highness's pardon," said Casperl, "but I am no prince."

"Oh, yes, you are!" said the Princess; "how did you come here, if you are not my True Prince? Didn't you come through the gate and across the tree, and haven't you driven the dragon away?"

"I only helped—" began Casperl.

"You did it all," said the Princess, "for I saw you. Please don't contradict a lady."

"But I don't see how I could—" Casperl began again.

"People who help others," said the Princess, "often

have a strength beyond their own. But perhaps you didn't come here to help me, after all?"

"Oh, your gracious Highness," cried Casperl, "there's nothing I wouldn't do to help you. But I'm sure I'm not a prince."

"And I am sure you are," said the Princess. She led him to a fountain near by, and when he looked at his reflection in the water, he saw that he was dressed more magnificently than any prince who ever yet had come to the enchanted mountain.

At that moment the wedding bells began to ring, and that is all I know of the fairy story, for Casperl and the Princess lived so happily ever after, in the castle on top of the mountain, that they never came down to tell the rest of it.

Tiger Woman

by ELEANORE M. JEWETT

NIM SAN had a large family of boys and girls, but no wife. Since his wife's death they had all lived with his mother, a gentle old lady who spoiled the children and could never say no to their desires. They had brass-studded chests filled with strings of money, each coin with a hole in its center so that a large number could be strung on a single cord. All Korean households kept their money in strings, and Nim San was fortunate in the length and number that he had stored away. He was a rich man. But there comes an end to all good material possessions if they are not replenished, and there came a time when the last string had been taken out of the last chest and there soon would not be a single coin left.

Nim San was dismayed, but not the children. They had always had everything they wanted and had never stopped to consider how or where their father had got it.

"Please, Honorable Parent," said one of the boys, "I shall need a new padded coat for the winter. Mine is much too short in the sleeves."

"We shall all need new coats for the New Year festival," cried the other boys.

"And new straw sandals, and wooden-soled boots for the rainy season—and soft shoes, too, with the toes turning up."

"And we need another kang-jar for kimchee—there are so many of us," the grandmother put in.

"And lots and lots of silk string and colored paper for our new kites," said the littlest boy.

"Honorable Father," one of the girls managed to put in her word in. "I am old enough for a jeweled comb and all of us need new ribbons." A chorus of "ye', ye' " came from all the little girls who had gathered around him. "We want— We want—"

"There are sweetmeats in Seoul better than our home-made ones—"

"Will you buy us—"

"Father, we need—"

Nim San threw up his hands in despair. "But, my children, there is no more money left!"

Silence followed for a few moments, then the chatter broke out again. "But, Honorable Father, we must have—" And so it went, more demanding than ever. Apparently nobody, not even Grandmother, could understand that without money there could be no more buying. Nim San tried to explain but at last gave it up and fled from the house, unable to bear the situation longer.

Not far from his home the mountains began. Their green wooded sides were showing patches of gold and s....let, russet and purple, for the autumn frosts were already tingling in the air, but Nim San had no eyes for the beauty around him. His heart was so heavy that he thought he might better die.

He climbed up and up, scarcely noticing where he was going, and when at last he roused himself from his sad thoughts and looked around, he realized that he was in a part of the country quite strange to him. He was not exactly lost, for the trail he had absent-mindedly followed was definite and wound on around the side of the hill and undoubtedly would lead him somewhere. Near him he noticed a small grass-roofed hut close to the steep mountain, and as he felt suddenly very weary, he walked over to it, pushed the bamboo door open and stepped inside. A light snow had begun to fall and he felt chilled to the very marrow of his bones. There being, of course, no heat inside the hut, it seemed damp and colder than outside, so he left the door open, sitting on the floor beside the high sill.

Before long he was astonished to see, coming up the trail toward him, a very beautiful sedan chair richly fitted out with silken hangings and borne by four runners in handsome livery. They came close to the hut and then paused, the bearers breathing heavily after their hard climb. Behind them at some distance an elderly woman in the customary dress of a servant followed, moving slowly and with difficulty, almost at the end of her strength.

The curtains of the chair parted and a woman looked out. Upon seeing Nim San she withdrew again in confusion, for it is not proper for a woman to be seen by any strange man, much less to converse with him. But after a moment she looked out again, motioned her bearers to set down the chair, and stepped out. She paid no attention

to Nim San but ran back to the old woman, put a support-
ing arm about her and led her into the hut. Nim San,
bowing courteously, moved aside and helped settle the
exhausted servant on the floor. Impulsively he took his
own padded coat off and laid it over her, for she was
shivering in spite of her layers of cotton clothing.

Then Nim San and the lady from the sedan chair looked
at each other. Never had he seen so beautiful or so unusual a face; young, with skin like palely tinted ivory, red
lips and delicate pointed chin, hair as black as midnight,
and thin black eyebrows. From under these her narrow
slanted eyes stared out at him—green like those of a cat.
Noticing his astonishment, the lady smiled faintly, and
Nim San was covered with confusion at his own rudeness.

"Honorable Lady," said he, bowing very low, "I ask a
thousand pardons. I—I—is there not something I can do
for you or for your woman? The snow is falling more
heavily now and already the evening chill has sharpened
the air—" He paused, scarcely knowing how to meet the
unblinking keenness of those green eyes.

"Thank you, good sir." The lady's voice was silken soft,
unlike any he had ever heard. "You have already shown
a remarkably unselfish kindness in placing your own coat

over my old nurse, but now you must put it on again before you are chilled through."

She clapped her hands and the bearers of the sedan came forward. Following her commands, they carried the old woman to the chair, laid her within it, and handed Nim San his coat again.

"And now," continued the lady, "I bid you follow after me. My house lies not many miles distant, in the heart of a hidden valley. There you will be welcome as my guest and can pass the night in warmth and comfort, and continue your journey in the morning." She climbed again into the sedan chair and drew the curtains. The runners picked up the poles and started at a jog trot, taking the trail farther into the mountains.

Nim San followed them. He had some difficulty in keeping their pace and soon fell behind, but in time he rounded a beetling bluff and came upon a narrow road leading straight down into a deep valley.

The snow had ceased falling and the air was tangy with the scent of evergreens. The sun came out and it seemed warmer as he descended. Then the pines and hemlocks gave place to trees whose flaming scarlet and gold vied with the sunset splendor of the western sky.

A large and beautiful palace stood directly in front of him, almost as fine and extensive as the emperor's own. Servants met him and took him to the men's apartment, where he bathed and put on the rich white silk apparel which they laid out for him. Then on a gold and lacquer tray his dinner was brought to him, served in shining brass bowls—rice and beans, fowl and kimchee and many special delicacies, all of the best and tastiest. He sat on his heels on the floor in front of the tray and, finding himself very hungry, made a good meal of it.

After the empty bowls and the spoons and chopsticks had been removed and he had washed his fingers in scented water, he was taken to the inner court, where he found the lady waiting to receive him. The old slave woman had evidently recovered for she sat crouched in a corner of the room, as motionless as a statue.

They had a pleasant evening together. The lady was gracious and friendly. She soon put him at his ease and he found himself telling of his motherless children, their continual but entirely understandable demands and his despair at being now unable to supply them.

The lady bade him lay aside his cares. "I live in this big house alone but for my old nurse and the other servants," she said. "There is no end to my wealth and my possessions, and most gladly will I give you all that you desire. To-morrow morning my servants will load a donkey for you with presents for your honorable mother and for the children, and strings of money for you to use as you have need. Only be my friend and come again to my palace when the winter evenings are long and cold. We will play at chess together and while away the long hours sitting here upon the warm floor. And always when you come I will supply all your needs for your home and family."

Nim San could do nothing but bow over and over again, murmuring his thanks while tears of relief and gratitude ran down his cheeks.

The next morning he found a donkey, laden with the gifts from the lady, standing in the courtyard. Servants stood about ready to serve him but he saw no sign of their mistress and at last left his good-bys and repeated thanks with the head man who promised to deliver them, and started on the long journey home.

The surprise and delight of his old mother and still more of his children can well be imagined and for a long time there were no demands from them. Nim San lived happily enough in the midst of his contented family, with money to spare and all their needs and desires satisfied. He thought often of the strange beautiful lady with the green eyes and her rich palace on the other side of the mountains and at length decided to visit her again as he had agreed to do.

He had no trouble in finding his way, though it was a long and difficult climb and bitter cold now that winter had set in. The lady seemed more lovely and charming than ever, and after that, all through the winter, he visited her again and yet again. Often she loaded him with gifts, but not always. Sometimes they would just spend a contented evening together playing chess or talking. He would sleep on a thick mat on the warm comfortable floor in the men's apartment and then go home the next morning without seeing her again and with no gifts or messages from her. He began to prefer not to be always indebted to her, for he realized that he loved her and wanted to make her his wife. The rich gifts he was constantly receiving from her, while he gave her nothing in return, made things awkward. Indeed the whole situation was awkward. There seemed to be no one who could act as a go-between for her, as is customary in all Korean marriages. Always the old nurse sat on her heels, motionless as a stone image, in the room with them, but there appeared to be no relative or proper person to whom his mother could go and discuss marriage for him.

Nim San was thinking about these things one day in early spring as he climbed the steep trail over the mountain. Suddenly he saw a strange white cloud rolling down upon him. It seemed like a huge soft ball so distinct and round that he expected to feel the impact of it as it fell upon him. He did not, however. It quietly surrounded him, shutting out instantly all sight of the valley beneath him and the tops of the hills above him and even the newly budding trees and bushes all around him. Mist, gray, thick, damp, cold, closed him in so completely that he stopped where he was, not daring to take a step forward or back.

Suddenly from somewhere above his head he heard a harsh voice saying, "Get down upon the ground, Nim San. Make reverent obeisance to the soul of your ancestor."

Nim San, trembling with terror, fell upon his knees, covering his eyes with his hands. "What would you, Great and Honorable Sir?" he said, touching his head to the earth nine times.

"I have come from the world beyond the farthest mountains to warn you," the voice continued. "Listen carefully to what I say and obey me."

There was a long moment of silence. Nim San, though still shaking with fear and astonishment, dropped his hands and looked about him. He could see nothing but the blank gray wall of mist. "Speak further, Honorable

Ancestor," said he tremblingly. "Your humble and dutiful descendant is listening."

"The woman you are bent upon visiting"—the voice was harsher than ever—"is no ordinary mortal, but a tiger. Did you not note the green eyes of her? Tiger-woman she is in very truth, permitted only for certain hours to take upon herself the form of a human."

Nim San gasped and then groaned. He had not realized the strength of his love for the lady but now the thought of losing her, of her being other than she seemed, cut his heart deeply and miserably.

"Waste no time in foolish sorrow," the voice went on in a cold, pitiless tone. "Go at once to the palace as you intended. Do not wait for the servants to admit you but thrust open the bamboo door of the inner court *without knocking*. Then you will see the lady of your love in her true and terrible state. What is more important, if you catch her in the act of changing herself into human form she will have to continue a beast, a fierce and hated tiger, forever."

With that the mist folded back like a blanket, rolled down the mountainside and disappeared.

For a few moments Nim San was too shocked and bewildered to move. Then he got to his feet and, without allowing himself time to think, hurried on. He reached the palace just as the half light was darkening into night, rushed through the outer court to the bamboo door of the women's apartment. He was about to thrust it open without knocking, as he had been bidden to do, when something stayed his hand. Though the green-eyed lady might indeed be a terrible tiger, able by some magic art to appear human and deceive him, he could not take a mean advantage over her. Many a time her strange eyes had looked into his with kindness, friendliness and even love. She had been good to him and to his children. He could not find it in his heart thus to betray her.

His hand dropped and he was about to turn away from the bamboo door when it slowly opened. The old nurse stood there and silently motioned him to come in. Then she left him and for some time he remained alone, standing with his hands in his sleeves, his head bowed.

She entered again, noiselessly. Nim San did not hear or see her come. But suddenly he found the lady with her standing in front of him, more beautiful and gracious than ever, tall, slim, in rich silken garments white as snow. Fearfully he looked into her face and cried out in his astonishment. Her eyes were no longer green but black and sparkling with joy and affection and—yes—amusement!

"Do not look so dumfounded, dear friend," said she, laughing. "All is as it should be. Come!" She led the way into the inner court and bade him sit beside her on the warm floor.

"You have this day saved me from a thousand years of grief and torment," she said. "In the spirit world I was condemned, for a sin I had committed, to take the form of a tiger for many generations. But every once in so often, for certain hours and certain days, it was permitted me to change into human form. If during my time as a woman I could win the love of a good man who, in spite of knowing my other state, would marry me, then I was to be allowed to stay human. There was one condition, however: neither he nor anyone must ever see me in the act of changing from tiger to woman or woman to tiger. If any mortal eyes should behold that great, mysterious act of magic, which none but the spirits that dwell beyond the farthest mountains know about or understand, then I would be condemned to keep my tiger shape unchanged for a thousand years, perhaps forever."

"So the soul of my ancestor spoke the truth," Nim San

murmured, "but not the whole truth, and I would rather have you as my wife, whatever shape or form you held in some past life, than any woman in this world or that Other."

The lady's black almond eyes grew soft and tears welled up in them. "You see," she said, brushing away the bright drops, "this proves I am altogether human, for neither beasts nor spirits, good or bad, can shed tears as humans do."

"But why should the soul of my ancestor counsel me to a deed of discourtesy and unkindness that would result only in sorrow to both of us?" Nim San was still puzzled.

"That was not the soul of your ancestor!" declared the lady. "It was an evil spirit that has long pursued me to destroy me, body and soul, forever. But now he can have no further power over me."

"Why is that?" asked Nim San, wondering.

"Because love is stronger than any evil," said the lady.

Now the rest of the story is easily guessed. Nim San married the lovely lady and took his children and his mother to the beautiful palace on the other side of the mountain. There they lived in great happiness together for the rest of their days.

The Swans of Ballycastle

by WALTER HACKETT

IN the Irish seaside town of Ballycastle, the people still tell the story of the three wandering swans. Everyone in this region knows it well, from the townspeople to the fishermen to the farmers.

Today the town looks much as it did hundreds of years ago. There is one main street that starts in the country and ends by the sea. At the far end of the town is a little harbor with a breakwater that protects the fishing boats from the stormings of the Irish Sea. Two small rivers— the Cary and the Shesk—twist their way through Ballycastle, past the whitewashed cottages with thatched roofs, finally emptying into the harbor. On the outskirts, where the green meadowland gradually becomes hills, then mountains, is a tower and beyond that a castle.

[259]

This is Ballycastle, the scene of the legend of the wandering swans.

There were three of them, a sister and two brothers. Only they actually weren't swans, but human beings. Deirdre, the oldest, was ten, Kevin was eight, and Michael was only five. Their father's name was Brian and he kept a small shop in the center of Ballycastle. The three children and their father lived on the second floor over the shop. Their mother had died when Michael was very young.

Brian, the father, raised the children as best he could. He wasn't unkind, nor did he purposely neglect them. But he was busy with his store, which sold a bit of almost everything.

For Deirdre, Kevin and Michael, it was something of a magic shop. On days when the rain slashed in from the sea and stormed down from the mountains, they used the store as a place to play. No matter what their game—housekeeper, farmer, fisherman, knight or lady—in their father's shop they found things to make the game more realistic.

The place where the three children liked best to play was on the beach by the harbor. This was long, wide and curving. They used the far corner, close by a small stone breakwater, where the water was calm and shallow and the white sand just right for building castles.

When they became tired of playing, they would scramble to the top of the breakwater and gaze out to sea. Straight ahead they would try to make out the small dot that was the Island of Rathlin.

"There is another island, a smaller one, on the far side of Rathlin," Deirdre told them. "It's not possible to see it from here."

"How do you know it actually is there?" Kevin asked.

"Because I have heard the fishermen speak of it. It's a small island, they say. Most of it is covered with trees."

"Does anyone live on it?" Michael asked.

"The fishermen say no."

"Do you suppose some day we may visit it?" Kevin wondered.

"Some day we may," his sister answered.

It was at this time that their father told them he was going to journey to Belfast to buy some goods for his shop. The news came as no surprise, for several times a year he made such a trip.

"If I remain away a bit longer than usual, have no

fear," he said. "I have arranged for the Widow Mac-Connell to run the shop and care for you."

"That isn't necessary, Father," Deirdre replied, "for I'm quite old enough to look after the three of us."

"And one of these days, the three of us will be old enough to tend the shop for you," Kevin said.

"Well, maybe that won't be necessary," Brian, their father, said slowly, a thoughtful look passing over his face. He left early the next morning, long before the sun removed from the mountains their night covering of purple.

In his absence, Widow MacConnell ran the shop and looked after the children. Not that she had much to do on that score, for Deirdre, as usual, took care of her young brothers. She cooked, served the meals, swept and dusted and saw that her brothers went to bed on time.

"You're a smart girl and a good one," the Widow Mac-Connell said to her.

Each night after supper, just before the sun slid over the edge of the distant mountains, the children would take a last look up the road leading to Belfast. They hoped to see their father driving his small cart and horse down the road toward home.

One morning the children rose and went downstairs. In the kitchen they found their father. With him was a strange woman. She was tall and thin and did not smile.

"I arrived home very early this morning," their father said. "You were still asleep."

He nodded toward the strange woman and said to the children, "This is your new mother."

The three children looked toward the strange woman, who stared back unsmilingly. "I was married while I was in Belfast," their father continued. "From now on, she'll look after you."

"But our real mother's gone away," Michael piped.

"I'm your mother now," the woman said sharply.

As soon as the children's father had left, she turned to them and stated, "Every day I'll have jobs for each of you. You're to do them well, or you'll be punished."

"Father's never punished us," Deirdre said. "He's had no need to, for all of us mind very well."

"We'll see about that. Now you, Deirdre, scrub the floor. You two boys carry in the logs for the fire."

"Please, but can't Michael do something easier?" Deirdre asked. "Those logs are awfully heavy for such a little fellow."

"You heard my orders," the woman snapped. "Obey them."

That night, while in bed, the children talked about this woman from Belfast, whom their father had married. Michael, exhausted from his unaccustomed heavy work, fell asleep murmuring, "I don't think I like her very much." The others lay awake.

"She shoved me," Kevin whispered, "and said I wasn't working hard enough. Why did Father have to marry her?"

His sister tried to assure him that their stepmother was not as bad as she seemed and that all of them would get to like her. Long after Kevin had joined Michael in sleep, Deirdre stared out of the window, watching the full moon ride higher and higher in the sky. No, she wasn't certain that she liked her stepmother, she told herself, but she must make every effort to do so.

In the days that followed, there were many changes in the once happy home and shop in Ballycastle. No longer were the children allowed to play on the floor of their father's store, nor could they touch the goods on the counters and shelves. No longer did they spend long and happy hours playing on the tiny protected beach.

Their lives became work and more work and no play.

Brian, the easy-going father, now that the children had a stepmother, paid even less attention to them. He was too busy, for his wife had told him that the way to become rich was to load his cart with goods and peddle them over the countryside to the people. And these trips meant that often several days went by without Deirdre and Kevin and Michael seeing him.

By this time, the stepmother, now sure of her position in the house and shop, thought nothing of punishing the children for wrongs she fancied they had done. Being a woman of short temper, many times she slapped them, and on other occasions, in a fit of rage, she would pack them off to bed with no supper.

One afternoon Deirdre discovered her brothers in the garret. They were staring out of the tiny window, trying to see the little island that lay on the other side of Rathlin, they told her. "But don't you know you can't see it, even when the day is clear?" she asked.

"I wish we could go there, all three of us, for good," Kevin said.

"Don't make such a strong wish, or it may come true," Deirdre warned him.

"I wish it would," he answered. "Then we'd be away from our stepmother and we'd be happy, just as we used to be."

On one of their father's frequent trips through the countryside a storm lashed in from the sea. Sweeping in over the harbor, it topped the stone breakwater and burst upon the town. The storm was so ferocious that the bell in the nearby church tower broke from the iron support and went crashing to the street below.

The children's stepmother was terrified and fled to her room, drawing the shutters in order to close out the cannon-like roaring of thunder and the howling of the wind. Meanwhile, Deirdre and her two brothers tried to put up the shutters on the shop windows. But the wind whisked the boards from their hands, and off they sailed like big pieces of flat paper. The sea, bursting over the beach, began to pour up the main street.

The three children worked to shut the heavy door, but the wind was too strong. And then the water, rolling faster and faster, swept into the open shop, forcing them to retreat up the stairs. The invading sea water soaked the bolts of cotton, silk and wool cloth and ruined the seed, flour, meat, fruit and vegetables.

The next morning Deirdre, Kevin and Michael were awakened by a bird singing outside their window. They jumped up from bed and looked out. The rain and wind had stopped and there was the brightest sun they had ever seen.

When they went downstairs and entered the shop, what a sight met their eyes! The entire contents of the room were on the floor, soaked through and through with rain and sea water. In the middle of the floor stood their stepmother, mumbling to herself about the damage.

As soon as she caught sight of the children, she advanced toward them, her eyes blazing like a pair of small fires. "And 'tis all the fault of you three!" she snapped. "Why did not you put up the shutters and close the door?"

"We tried, but we weren't strong enough," Deirdre answered. "If you had helped us we might have saved the goods."

"I'll tell your father it was all your fault."

"We'll tell him the truth," Deirdre said, "for it's time you stopped blaming us for things we didn't do."

"Get out of here!" the stepmother stormed. With that she chased them into the littered street.

"I've hated you from the moment I set eyes on you!" she screamed. "I hope never to see you again!"

"It's almost a curse you're drawing upon us," Deirdre said.

"If it isn't, I'll make it one!" their stepmother screeched. "I'll send you three away from here." She pointed to the bell that now lay shattered on the ground. "May you not return until the sound of that bell, restored to the belfry, reaches your ears!"

The speechless children wandered down the street. They went past the harbor road and along the meadows, following the winding course of the Cary River. A long time later, they dropped to the low-lying riverbank, tired from their walk.

It was peaceful and quiet. Downstream the children saw a pair of white swans floating along the river's surface.

"If only we could go to the little island that lies beyond Rathlin," Kevin said wistfully.

"But how could we ever travel there?" Deirdre asked.

Michael suddenly pointed to the swans down river. "If we were like those swans, we could swim to the island!" he said excitedly. "That's what I'd like us to be—beautiful

William Pène du Bois

white swans living on the little island we've never seen!"

"So do I!" Deirdre cried. "Then we'd be happy."

While saying this, she looked into the clear water of the river. And what she saw made her start. The reflection that stared up at her was that of a swan. Quickly she looked at herself and her two brothers. She had become a

white swan and so had they. They were smaller than human beings, but Kevin was still bigger than Michael and Deirdre was bigger than both.

"Look, I'm a swan!" Kevin cried. "And I have wings instead of hands, and my feet are webbed!"

"Now we can fly," Michael said excitedly, flapping his

wide white wings. As he did so, he fell into the river, where he swam in tight little circles, like a sailboat without a rudder. The other two immediately slid into the water and chugged around, testing their newly found skill.

Kevin and Michael then looked to their sister for guidance, as they had always done.

"It's going to be a long trip to our new home," she said. "I will lead the way."

They paddled down the river, past the green meadowland and into the tiny harbor of Ballycastle. Like a small white fleet of ships, they changed their course and churned straight out into the sea toward the distant Island of Rathlin.

Late the next morning, the three children sailed past the Island of Rathlin, which seemed to float on top of the water like a gray-black whale. As they skirted Rathlin, they suddenly saw stretched out before them another island, only this one was small and green and was covered with trees of all sizes and shapes.

"Do you think this is our island?" Kevin asked anxiously.

"I do hope so," Michael complained, "for my feet are

tired from paddling, and it's hungry I am. I had no supper last night."

They swam closer and just before they were ready to go into what appeared to be the main harbor, a swan—the largest one they had ever seen—paddled over to them. The children waited, not knowing what to expect. Indeed, they were a bit frightened.

Suddenly the strange swan called out to them in a deep voice, "Welcome. Welcome to the Happy Island Where Time Stands Still."

"Good morning, sir," Deirdre faltered.

"And the top of the morning to you, Deirdre."

"You know my name?" she asked, surprised.

"Indeed I do," the swan replied. "And behind you is Kevin, and bringing up the rear is little Michael. Welcome, one and all." Then he continued, "Allow me to introduce myself. I'm Rory."

"But Mr. Rory, how do you know our names?" Deirdre asked.

"Because word was sent to me yesterday that you would be on your way," came the reply.

"And how is it, Mr. Rory, that you can speak, just like a real person?" Kevin asked.

"Because I once was a 'real person,' as you put it, a grown man."

"Have you lived here very long?" asked Deirdre.

"Over one hundred years," the swan answered.

"Indeed, you must be very old," Michael commented.

"Actually I'm only twenty-eight years old," Rory replied.

The children were too astonished to speak. Then Rory told them the story of the Happy Island Where Time Stands Still. The island was especially reserved for people who, in the outside world, had led unhappy lives through no fault of their own. The people who lived here, like the four of them, had also been changed into white swans.

No one was unhappy on the island, Rory explained, and no one ever grew old, but always remained the same age he had been when he had become a swan. However, only those who deserved it were admitted.

"Suppose a person wants to leave here?" Deirdre asked. "Can he do so?"

"Certainly," Rory said. "Only no one has ever wanted to leave."

When they landed on the island, Rory introduced the

newcomers to the other swans, who had been waiting patiently to meet them.

After a few days, Deirdre and her brothers settled down to live in their new home. Rory showed each how to build a nest of twigs, branches, leaves and grass. The children located their soft beds within a cluster of trees.

During the days, Deirdre, Kevin and Michael—like the other swans—gathered food and did their share of work to keep the island tidy. Although time passed, none of the swans realized it, including Deirdre, Kevin and Michael. There were no clocks to tick away the minutes and hours and no calendars to show the passing of days, weeks, months and years.

On one warm summer afternoon the three children climbed the small knoll in the center of the island in their search for food. Soon a wind sprang up and, riding on its heels, was a faint but persistent sound. Deirdre stopped in her tracks and listened. The sound stopped. Then it began again, this time louder. "Listen!" she called to her brothers. "Listen to the sound!"

They looked at each other in surprise.

"It's a bell," Kevin whispered.

"Yes, a bell," Deirdre said, "the bell from the church that stands near our old home."

"But that can't be so," Michael interrupted. "During that fearful storm, was it not blown to the ground, where it broke?"

As the sound of the bell continued to reach them, they thought of the curse their stepmother had called down upon them. Her words came back, "May you not return until the sound of that bell, restored to the belfry, reaches your ears!"

"What are we to do?" Kevin asked.

"It means we must return to Ballycastle," Deirdre said slowly.

"But I don't want to go back," Michael complained.

"We've never been so happy," Kevin added.

"We have no choice but to return to Ballycastle," their sister explained. "The bell is telling us that the curse of our stepmother has been lifted and that we are free."

That night Deirdre spoke to Rory and explained what had happened. He told her he, too, had heard the bell, and he knew what its ringing meant. Whether or not she and her brothers returned to Ballycastle, he explained, must be their choice.

In the morning all the swans walked with Deirdre, Kevin and Michael to the edge of the water. Although everyone tried to be cheerful, there was great sadness.

"Always remember you are free to return," Rory said. "I am sure you will come back to us. And every day we will watch for you."

"Bon voyage!" everyone cried as the three swans swam away from the Happy Island Where Time Stands Still.

Aided by a favoring wind, the children made fine time. However, it was very late at night when they landed at Ballycastle. They walked to the small protected beach where they had once built castles from sand. Exhausted, they fell into a dreamless sleep, lying close to each other to keep warm.

Deirdre was awakened by the screeching gulls, winging and dipping over the harbor. She stretched a bit, and, as she tried to ruffle her feathers, she was so surprised that she could make no sound. In place of her feathers was skin. Her wings were now arms and hands, and her webbed feet had been replaced by legs and toes. Not only had she regained her human form, but she was dressed in exactly the same clothes she had worn before becoming a swan. She darted a look at her sleeping brothers. They, too, were human beings again, and were dressed as they had been in the past.

When she shook them from their sleep, their surprise was greater than her own. The most amazing thing was that none of them had changed. Michael was still five years old, Kevin was eight, and Deirdre was ten.

They were talking among themselves when a voice was heard to say, "And what would you be doing sitting here on the beach so early in the morning?"

They looked up. Standing over them was a big, pleasant-faced young man. He had a twinkle in his eye, a broad smile on his face, and his hair was as red as the brightest of sunsets. "Are you perhaps not lost?" he went on. "Certainly you are strangers to this village, for I live here and never before have I seen you."

"We're not exactly strangers to Ballycastle—" Deirdre began.

"Indeed we're not," Michael piped. "We live here." Before he could say anything else, his sister nudged him into silence.

"We don't truly live here," Deirdre explained, "but we've been here before, quite some time ago, I should say."

"Where are your parents?" the young man asked.

"Our mother is dead, and we don't exactly know where our father is at the moment," Deirdre replied.

"Could it be then that you're the children of wandering gypsies, who have left you behind?" the young man asked.

"No, our father owns a shop," Deirdre answered.

Upon learning their names, he informed them that he was the local schoolmaster, by the name of Shane Mac-Connell, and that he lived alone.

"Are you perhaps related to the Widow MacConnell?" asked Kevin.

He shook his head. "I'm the only MacConnell left in the village. Are you certain you're thinking of Bally-castle?"

"Oh, very certain," Kevin said. "The Widow Mac-Connell lives on the main road directly across from the church."

A look of wonderment passed quickly over the young schoolmaster's face. Then he said, "Well, while you are in Ballycastle, you must stay at my small cottage. And don't say no, for you can't sleep on the beach like three sea gulls."

"Or swans," Michael added.

[279]

Whistling a cheerful tune, Shane MacConnell led them from the beach and along the main road of Ballycastle. With the exception of a few new houses and a few old ones that had been torn down, the village looked much the same as when the children had left it.

If anything, it was the people who had changed. Deirdre, Kevin and Michael did not recognize one familiar face. The villagers, they noticed, also wore a type of clothing different from that which the children remembered. A boy glanced up and, pointing a finger, yelled, "Now look at those three young ones, will you! Did you ever see such clothes? They must be from another land." A quick look from the schoolmaster made the village boy stop his hooting.

"We are dressed differently than these children," Deirdre said.

"Ah, sure, don't let that bother you," the schoolmaster answered. "They don't know any better, never having traveled one step from Ballycastle."

He stopped in front of a house. "This is my home," he said. It was the same house where the children's old friend, the Widow MacConnell, had lived.

Without thinking, the children walked a few steps

farther until they stood outside their old home. It no
longer was a shop. Instead, it was a home, complete with
furniture and pictures on the walls. Two small children
were playing on the floor, while their mother, seated in a
chair, was sewing.

Three questions popped into each of their minds. What

had happened to their father? Where was their stepmother? Why was the shop no longer a shop?

Next they examined the church across the road. Their eyes went up and up to the belfry, and, as they looked, the bell tolled the hour. Yes, the children thought, that surely was the same bell which had called them back to Ballycastle, the very bell that had shattered to the ground during the storm.

"The bell has a sweet voice, don't you think?" asked the schoolmaster. "Only two days ago it was put back in the belfry. I was the one who discovered it, lying useless in a nearby shed."

"The bell was broken in two!" cried young Michael. "Dashed to the ground by the anger of the storm."

That night, exhausted from their busy day, the children crawled into a big feather bed in the house that had once sheltered the Widow MacConnell, their old friend. No sooner had Shane MacConnell said good night and disappeared down the small twisting staircase, than Kevin and Michael fell sound asleep.

Before Deirdre closed her eyes, one question kept going through her mind. Was the schoolmaster at all puzzled over the sudden appearance of his three young guests?

The Swans of Ballycastle

The schoolmaster at that very moment was asking himself the same thing. Yes, indeed, he was most puzzled. Where had the children come from? They obviously knew their way around the village, for they had pointed out to him the lanes, the meadows and the two rivers. They knew all about the old tower and the castle that sat on the nearby hill.

However, it was most strange, the young schoolmaster thought, that the three children knew no one in the village. That afternoon they had passed some of the village people, and not a word of greeting had been spoken. The villagers had stared at them, and Deirdre, Kevin, and Michael had stared back.

Then there was the subject of the bell. How had young Michael known it had been dashed to the ground, broken in two by the worst storm Ballycastle had ever experienced?

"Well, 'tis surely a mystery," Shane said aloud, "and one I can't solve, at least not tonight." He tapped out the ashes in his pipe, put out the lamp and went to bed.

Before he fell asleep, he made a promise to himself to solve the puzzle.

In the days of the green summer that followed, Shane,

the schoolmaster, was able to spend much time with his young friends. He took them on walks, on picnics and for rides by horse and cart through the countryside.

Once he took them swimming in the harbor, and, to his surprise, each of the children very easily outswam him, a skill they had picked up while they were swans. In fact, the swan habit was still so strong that young Michael often insisted upon upending himself, sticking his head under water and looking for food in the bottom of the harbor!

As the bright summer days winged by, the children spent more and more time with Shane. The village children obviously didn't like to play with Deirdre, Kevin and Michael and became strangely silent every time the three newcomers approached. When some of the parents asked Shane who his young guests were and where they came from, he was quite abrupt, saying they were friends who had come for a visit.

One cool evening, while Shane and the three children were sitting before the open fire, he made a remark. "School will be starting very soon, and so you will become my students. That will be grand fun for all of us."

The children didn't answer. Instead, they continued

to stare into the dancing flames, their thoughts far away.

The next day Shane rode his horse down the road toward Belfast. In a deep glen he called upon Finn, the best story-teller in that entire section. Finn was old, so old that he didn't exactly know his age. But he had a remarkable mem-ory, and he knew the history and folk tales of the region as no other man. Shane spent a long time with old Finn, and when he mounted his horse and galloped along the road to Ballycastle, the long evening shadows had settled over the dark glen.

The next night there was a hint of storm in the air. After the children had finished their supper, Shane said he had a story to tell, and so all four took their places in front of the fireplace.

"The story took place many years ago," Shane be-gan, "and its starts right here in Ballycastle. According to the tale, it seems there were three children . . ." And then Shane told them the whole account of their own lives.

"We thought you would find out," Deirdre said.

"And now that you know who we are, perhaps you don't like us," Michael frowned.

"I like you better than before," Shane smiled, "for I know that you must be rather lonely."

"You haven't told us what happened to our father and stepmother," Deirdre said.

The schoolmaster related how their father, upon his return, had learned that his wife had driven the children from the house. Accordingly, he had sent her back to Belfast away from his sight forever. He called down upon his own head the wrath of heaven for having been so neglectful a father.

After a number of years he sold the shop and disappeared from Ballycastle. Years later word reached the village that he had died.

The children then told him about the Happy Island Where Time Stands Still, about Rory and the other people who live there in the form of swans.

"You do believe our story?" Deirdre asked.

"And why would I not believe it?" he questioned smiling. "Did you not return after all these years?"

He looked into the flames of the fire. "It must be a wonderful place, this island of yours. I should like to see it."

"Oh, but you can't," Kevin said, "for it is only for people who have led unhappy lives, and you, Mr. Shane, you lead a very happy life."

"But what of you three?" Shane asked. "Will you remain here with me?"

When they didn't answer, he went on. "The only way that you can turn into swans again is to have another storm take place at the same time of day, just as before. And with it the bell in our church must again be hurled to the ground and lie there broken. Only then, if the desire in you is strong enough, will you become white swans, free to return to your island."

It was with this thought that he sent them off to bed.

The wind, which howled through most of the night, came to a protesting stop by the time the children finished their breakfast the next morning. Shane said that he had an errand to do at the village of Larne and would return by late afternoon. They stood in the road and waved good-by to him as he galloped away.

Shortly after this, the sky blackened. The placid water in the harbor turned into waves that grew bigger by the hour. When Deirdre saw the storm develop, she and her brother closed the shutters on Shane's house and bolted the doors. Through a chink in one of the shutters, they watched as the water, pouring in from the harbor, began flooding the main street.

At the very height of the storm, the children heard a grinding sound, followed by a heavy crash and a strange noise, as though caused by a protesting bell. No sooner had this happened than the storm ended. They unbolted the door and threw it open. The water was quickly retracing its course to the harbor. The sun was out, and the sky was clear.

Deirdre pointed to the middle of the road. The church bell, ripped from the belfry, lay shattered on the ground.

"It's just as before," Michael whispered.

"We're free to return now," Deirdre said.

Without another word, the children walked down the street, with Michael in the middle, his hand held tightly by his sister. They walked slowly but surely past the harbor and toward the winding Cary River.

It was late afternoon when Shane returned from Larne. When he reached his house, he dashed inside. His voice echoed hollowly through the emptiness when he called out, "Children! Deirdre! Kevin! Michael" He went from room to room, but there was no sign of them.

Shane went out into the street but stopped suddenly. It was then that he saw the broken church bell. Mounting his horse, he drummed down the road, past the harbor, along the river bank, calling out to the children as he rode. But no answer came back.

When he returned to the harbor, he had one of the local fishermen sail him out beyond the breakwater toward the Island of Rathlin. The schoolmaster stood in the prow of the small boat, his eyes sweeping the sea. They sailed for several hours, until suddenly the fisherman yelled to Shane. Pointing ahead, he passed Shane a spyglass.

Shane clapped the glass to his eye. Far ahead, the rays of the late sun had opened a bright path over the water. Directly in its center, he could see three white swans swimming steadily forward, setting a course for just beyond the Island of Rathlin. A sad look passed over his face, which was quickly replaced by a faint smile, then a wide grin.

"Do you see anything?" the fisherman called out.

Shane slowly put down the glass and turned to the fisherman.

"Bring her around and head for home," he said. "I've found what I was searching for."

Two of Everything

by ALICE RITCHIE

Mr. and Mrs. Hak-Tak were rather old and rather poor. They had a small house in a village among the mountains and a tiny patch of green land on the mountain side. Here they grew the vegetables which were all they had to live on, and when it was a good season and they did not need to eat up everything as soon as it was grown, Mr. Hak-Tak took what they could spare in a basket to the next village, which was a little larger than theirs, and sold it for as much as he could get. Then he bought some oil for their lamp, and fresh seeds, and every now and then, but not often, a piece of cotton stuff to make new coats and trousers for himself and his wife. You can imagine they did not often get the chance to eat meat.

Now, one day it happened that when Mr. Hak-Tak was digging in his precious patch, he unearthed a big brass pot.

He thought it strange that it should have been there for so long without his having come across it before, and he was disappointed to find that it was empty; still, he thought they would find some use for it, so when he was ready to go back to the house in the evening he decided to take it with him. It was very big and heavy, and in his struggles to get his arms round it and raise it to a good position for carrying, his purse, which he always took with him in his belt, fell to the ground. To be quite sure he had it safe, he put it inside the pot and so staggered home with his load.

As soon as he got into the house Mrs. Hak-Tak hurried from the inner room to meet him.

"My dear husband," she said, "whatever have you got there?"

"For a cooking-pot it is too big; for a bath a little too small," said Mr. Hak-Tak. "I found it buried in our vegetable patch and so far it has been useful in carrying my purse home for me."

"Alas," said Mrs. Hak-Tak," something smaller would have done as well to hold any money we have or are likely to have," and she stooped over the pot and looked into its dark inside.

As she stooped, her hairpin—for poor Mrs. Hak-Tak

had only one hairpin for all her hair and it was made of carved bone—fell into the pot. She put in her hand to get it out again, and then she gave a loud cry which brought her husband running to her side.

"What is it?" he asked. "Is there a viper in the pot?"

"Oh, my dear husband," she cried. "What can be the meaning of this? I put my hand into the pot to fetch out my hairpin and your purse, and look, I have brought out two hairpins and two purses, both exactly alike."

"Open the purse. Open both purses," said Mr. Hak-Tak. "One of them will certainly be empty."

But not a bit of it. The new purse contained exactly the same number of coins as the old one—for that matter, no one could have said which was the new and which the old—and it meant, of course, that the Hak-Taks had exactly twice as much money in the evening as they had had in the morning.

"And two hairpins instead of one!" cried Mrs. Hak-Tak, forgetting in her excitement to do up her hair which was streaming over her shoulders. "There is something quite unusual about this pot."

"Let us put in the sack of lentils and see what happens," said Mr. Hak-Tak. He, too, was becoming excited.

They heaved in the bag of lentils and when they pulled it out again—it was so big it almost filled the pot—they saw another bag of exactly the same size waiting to be pulled out in its turn. So now they had two bags of lentils instead of one.

"Put in the blanket," said Mr. Hak-Tak. "We need another blanket for the cold weather." And, sure enough, when the blanket came out, there lay another behind it.

"Put my wadded coat in," said Mr. Hak-Tak, "and then when the cold weather comes there will be one for you as well as for me. Let us put in everything we have in turn. What a pity we have no meat or tobacco, for it seems that the pot cannot make anything without a pattern."

Then Mrs. Hak-Tak, who was a woman of great intelligence, said, "My dear husband, let us put the purse in again and again and again. If we take two purses out each time we put one in, we shall have enough money by tomorrow evening to buy everything we lack."

"I am afraid we may lose it this time," said Mr. Hak-Tak, but in the end he agreed, and they dropped in the purse and pulled out two. Then they added the new money to the old and dropped it in again and pulled out the larger amount twice over. After a while the floor was covered with old leather purses and they decided just to throw the money in by itself. It worked quite as well and saved trouble; every time, twice as much money came out as went in, and every time they added the new coins to the old and threw them all in together. It took them some hours to tire of this game, but at last Mrs. Hak-Tak said, "My dear husband, there is no need for us to work so hard. We shall see to it that the pot does not run away, and we can always make more money as we want it. Let us tie up what we have."

It made a huge bundle in the extra blanket and the Hak-Taks lay and looked at it for a long time before they slept. They talked of all the things they would buy and the improvements they would make in the cottage.

The next morning they rose early. Mr. Hak-Tak filled a wallet with money from the bundle and set off for the big village to buy more things in one morning than he had bought in a whole fifty years.

Mrs. Hak-Tak saw him off and then she tidied up the cottage and put the rice on to boil. Then she had another look at the bundle of money, and made herself a whole set of new hairpins from the pot. Next she made twenty candles instead of the one which was all they had possessed up to now. After that she slept for a while, having been up so late the night before. But just before the time when her husband should be back, she awoke and went over to the pot. She dropped in a cabbage leaf to make sure it was still working properly, and when she took two leaves out she sat down on the floor and put her arms round it.

"I do not know how you came to us, my dear pot," she said, "but you are the best friend we ever had."

Then she knelt to look inside it, and at that moment her husband came to the door. Turning quickly to see all the wonderful things he had bought, she overbalanced and fell into the pot.

Mr. Hak-Tak put down his bundles and ran across and caught her by the ankles to pull her out. But, oh, mercy, no sooner had he set her carefully on the floor than he saw the kicking legs of another Mrs. Hak-Tak in the pot! What was he to do? Well, he could not leave her there, so he caught her ankles and pulled, and another Mrs. Hak-Tak so exactly like the first that no one would have told one from the other, stood beside them.

"Here's an extraordinary thing," said Mr. Hak-Tak, looking helplessly from one to the other.

"I will not have a second Mrs. Hak-Tak in the house!"
screamed the old Mrs. Hak-Tak.

All was confusion. The old Mrs. Hak-Tak shouted and
wrung her hands and wept, Mr. Hak-Tak was scarcely

calmer, and the new Mrs. Hak-Tak sat down on the floor as if she knew no more than they did what was to happen next.

"One wife is all I want," said Mr. Hak-Tak, "but how could I have left her in the pot?"

"Put her back in it again!" cried Mrs. Hak-Tak.

"What? And draw out two more?" said her husband. "If two wives are too many for me, what should I do with three? No! No!" He stepped back quickly as if he was stepping away from the three wives and, missing his footing, lo and behold, *he* fell into the pot!

Both Mrs. Hak-Taks ran and each caught an ankle and pulled him out and set him on the floor, and there, oh, mercy, was another pair of kicking legs in the pot! Again each caught hold of an ankle and pulled, and soon another Mr. Hak-Tak, so exactly like the first that no one could have told one from the other, stood beside them.

Now the old Mr. Hak-Tak liked the idea of his double no more than Mrs. Hak-Tak had liked the idea of hers. He stormed and raged and scolded his wife for pulling him out of the pot, while the new Mr. Hak-Tak sat down on the floor beside the new Mrs. Hak-Tak and looked as if, like her, he did not know what was going to happen next.

Then the old Mrs. Hak-Tak had a very good idea. "Listen, my dear husband," she said, "now, do stop scolding and listen, for it is really a good thing that there is a new one of you as well as a new one of me. It means that you and I can go on in our usual way, and these new people, who are ourselves and yet not ourselves, can set up house together next door to us."

And that is what they did. The old Hak-Taks built themselves a fine new house with money from the pot, and they built one just like it next door for the new couple. They all lived together in the greatest friendliness, because, as Mrs. Hak-Tak said, "The new Mrs. Hak-Tak is really more than a sister to me, and the new Mr. Hak-Tak is really more than a brother to you."

The neighbors were very much surprised, both at the sudden wealth of the Hak-Taks and at the new couple who resembled them so strongly that they must, they thought, be very close relations of whom they had never heard before. They said: "It looks as though the Hak-Taks, when they so unexpectedly became rich, decided to have two of everything, even of themselves, in order to enjoy their money more."

About the Child Study Association of America

The Child Study Association of America is a nonprofit organization which for the past seventy years has been carrying on a program to help parents bring up their children wisely, with enjoyment, and with full use of the best knowledge available. Its publications, including the quarterly magazine, *Child Study,* are widely distributed in this country and abroad. Its Children's Book Committee offers guidance to parents in the selection of children's books. The Committee reviews all the current books as they are published and issues an annual list of its selections.

Out of the Committee's long years of experience have come a number of story collections: *Read-to-Me Storybook, Read Me Another Story, Read Me More Stories, Read-to-Yourself Storybook, More Read-to-Yourself Stories: Fun and Magic,* and *Holiday Storybook.*

About William Pène du Bois

William Pène du Bois was born in New Jersey and educated in this country and France. In his studio just off Times Square, which is bathed alternately in red and green neon light, he writes and illustrates wonderful books that have excited children everywhere. He is the author of *Lion; Bear Party; The Giant; The Twenty-One Balloons,* which won the Newbery Medal in 1948; *The Adventures of Otto,* and many others.

Mr. Pène du Bois also writes plays and designs extraordinary sea monsters and dragons for the theater and cinema. He is married to the artist and stage designer, Willa Kim.